WRITING AIN'T FOR SISSIES

By

ERINA BRIDGET RING

ISBN-10: 0-692-79515-4
ISBN-13: 978-0-692-79515-6

Cover design by Rae Monet
Edited by Carolyn Woolston
Formatted by Self-Publishing Services LLC. (www.Self-Publishing-Service.com)

For Jack

We walk side by side

Acknowledgments

I would like to thank my family and friends who gave their support, especially Barbara Heppe, Coleen McCluskey, Paula Phillips, Tamara Pieri, Beverly Smith-Mediavilla, and Lisa Winograde. Finally, thanks to my editor and friend Carolyn Woolston, without whose expertise my stories would not have made it onto the printed page.

Chapter One

High Anxiety

"It's done! My manuscript is finished!" Clara jumped up and rushed down the hallway to the kitchen. "Honey, I just finished my memoir!"

Trey looked up from his morning coffee. "That's great, Clara. I can't wait to tell the family."

Clara stopped in her tracks. "Oh, no! Not yet. Let me get it sent off to the printer. Then I'll decide how to tell them about it."

Her husband's eyebrows went up. Trey knew she'd been writing some kind of memoir, but he hadn't seen any of it. "Did you spill any family secrets?" he joked.

She clutched the manuscript pages close to her chest and without a word walked back into her tiny office. The memoir was full of carefully recalled details she remembered from her childhood, trips in the family car, moving into new houses, going to school, conversations, everything.

How am I going to tell my family that I've written about all of us? She sucked in a breath. Maybe they won't even be interested in reading it. But later, after it's printed, someone might see it in the bookstore, and they would be curious.

Suddenly her heart started to race.

*   *   *

That evening Aunt Sarah invited Clara and Trey to dinner. On the way to her aunt's house, Clara laid her hand on Trey's arm. "Please don't say anything about my memoir. There's a lot of personal stuff in there, and I'm feeling a little uneasy about revealing so much about myself. Besides, Aunt Sarah's always been funny about things like that."

"Sure. Okay."

But when they sat down to dinner the first words out of his mouth were, "Guess what? Your niece just finished her memoir!"

Clara slipped her hand under the table and touched his thigh.

"What's wrong?" he said quietly.

She leaned in close and whispered, "I asked you not to mention my book!"

Her husband nodded, but it was too late. Aunt Sarah was staring at her.

"What did you write about in your memoir, Clara?"

Clara cleared her throat. "Oh, just about growing up in New Millhaven. You know, about school and the kids I played with. It was a challenge to remember it all."

Aunt Sarah reached over and clasped Clara's hand. "I don't think you should publish such a book, Clara. It would be a shame to talk about things that should never be revealed."

"What?"

"You know what I mean, Clara. Some things should never be mentioned in public."

Clara frowned. "What things? What are you talking about?"

"Oh, just … things."

So Aunt Sarah didn't approve of the fact that she'd written a memoir. But she hadn't read any of it! What was her aunt so apprehensive about?

When dinner was over, Clara and Trey drove home in silence. "Trey, talking about my memoir makes me nervous," she said. "Please don't mention it to anyone else before it's published."

"Oh. Okay."

Upstairs in the bedroom, she stood for a long time in front of the mirror. How dare Aunt Sarah tell her what she should or shouldn't write about! Her memoir wasn't about her aunt; it was about herself! About *her* life, not Aunt Sarah's.

The following day Clara made an appointment with Dr. Shu to talk about the anxiety she'd felt at dinner. Just before she left, Trey found her staring at herself in the mirror.

"Honey? What's wrong?"

"Oh … I guess it's nothing. Aunt Sarah is really upset about my memoir for some reason, and that's made me even more apprehensive about publishing it."

7

"Has she read it?"

"No, she hasn't. No one has."

"Then I say forget about Aunt Sarah. You just go ahead with your publishing project. It's your memoir, not hers."

* * *

She wanted to tell her doctor about the anxiety she was feeling, about her heart pounding at odd times and feeling short of breath on the way home last night. She drove slowly to his office, which was located at the end of a winding road, wedged between two Victorian houses now used as professional offices.

She found a parking space on Third Avenue, right in front of the building.

Inside the office, Dr. Shu walked into the room where Clara waited, smiling as he always did. He was tall and soft-spoken, and he stayed on top of developments in medicine. He'd been Clara's doctor for years, and he knew her well.

"Clara! How are you?"

Clara tried to smile. "I'm fine," she started to say. But all at once the room started to spin, and she couldn't catch her breath.

"Clara? What's the matter?"

She couldn't say a word, and then she was sobbing.

Dr. Shu grabbed the telephone on the wall. "Nurse," he snapped into the receiver. Before she knew it she was lying on the exam table, and people started hooking her up to an EKG monitor.

"Clara, just breathe normally."

After what seemed like hours, he shooed the nurses out and said she could sit up. "You're not having a heart attack, Clara. What you had just now was a panic attack."

"But …"

"What's upsetting you?" he asked quietly.

"I'm not really sure," she began. "It started last night, when my husband and I were having dinner with my aunt."

"And?"

She thought for a minute. "Well," she said slowly, "I have just finished writing a personal memoir and I'm getting criticized for doing it."

"Is it a tell-all kind of book?" Dr. Shu asked.

"No, it isn't. It's just about when I was growing up. But last night at dinner my aunt said I shouldn't have written it."

"Do you really care what your aunt thinks?"

Clara blew her nose into a Kleenex. "Not really, I guess. I've never written anything before, especially not anything about myself. I've really been a private person, just focused on being a good wife and a good mother for my kids. Last night my aunt made me feel like I'm doing something wrong."

Dr. Shu fished in his pocket and handed her a business card. "I want you to call this person, Clara. She's a therapist. I advise you to talk your feelings over with her, and in the meantime, try to put this in perspective. Remember, you know better than anyone else what is right or wrong for you."

Ten minutes later Clara stood in front of the medical building, gripping the card with a name and phone number on it. Susan Morrison, Psychotherapist.

She called the number and got an answering machine; she couldn't think what to say, so she hung up. What should she say to a therapist's answering machine? What she wanted to say was that she was a woman in her fifties and she thought she was losing her mind, but she guessed that didn't make much sense.

Later she tried Dr. Morrison's number again and once more got the answering machine. This time she had rehearsed what to say. "This is Clara Perkins. Dr. Arthur Shu suggested I call you because … because …"

For a moment she couldn't finish the sentence. "Please call me back at your earliest convenience."

There! She'd taken the first step toward figuring out what was going on with her. She drove to the market, where she bought salmon and salad makings for dinner, then to the coffee shop for a doughnut and a latte. She sat alone at the table for an hour, trying to convince herself everything was fine.

That night she crawled into bed next to Trey and decided to tell him what Dr. Shu had said. "Honey, do you know what a panic attack is?"

"Yeah, he said. "What about it?"

"I had one today, in the doctor's office."

"A panic attack? Oh, honey." He pulled her close.

"I think it had something to do with my memoir."

He frowned. "Was it about what Aunt Sarah said? I didn't realize that upset you so much."

"Dr. Shu recommended a therapist. He says it's best to talk it over with a professional."

"What did the therapist say?"

"I haven't talked to her yet. Apparently she doesn't answer her phone very often, because I left two messages today and she hasn't called me back yet."

*   *   *

The next morning, Clara was sitting at the kitchen table when Trey walked in, looking handsome in his blue suit and red-striped tie. His dark brown hair was turning gray at the temples, which gave him a distinguished look. She poured him a cup of coffee.

"Are you seeing clients this morning?"

He nodded. "What are you up to today?"

She sighed. She hadn't slept much last night and she hoped he wouldn't notice how jangled her nerves were. "I need to decide on the cover for the book."

Trey grinned. "Ah, now it's 'the' book, is it?"

She gave him a sidelong glance and tried to smile. "I guess so. For sure it's 'the' book that's got Aunt Sarah all upset."

"Clara, if I were you I'd try not to worry about Aunt Sarah. Personally I can't wait to read your memoir." He kissed her goodbye and walked out the front door on the way to his office.

Chapter Two
The Appointment

For her first appointment with Dr. Morrison, Clara wore a pair of perfectly creased black wool slacks and a crisp white shirt. Her straight brunette hair lay on her shoulders and she tucked the sides behind her ears, applied pale rose lipstick, and pinched her cheeks for some color. Around her neck she fastened her favorite piece of jewelry, a simple but elegant gold necklace Trey had given her on their 20th wedding anniversary.

She drove through town with growing apprehension. She had never talked to a therapist before, and she didn't know what to expect. Would she get along with this Dr. Morrison? Could this person help her deal with the anxiety she was feeling?

She parked the white Volvo on Merritt Street in front of Susan Morrison's office, a one-story brown building that looked like a house, and walked apprehensively to the front door.

The floor creaked in the small waiting room. Two people raised their heads, then quickly averted their eyes. The younger woman was talking on her cell phone; the older woman was reading a magazine. Clara noticed that the beige tweed carpet was worn. Five diplomas hung on the white-painted wall, each for a different doctor. Susan Morrison's diploma, from Cornell University, needed straightening.

Clara took a seat on a straight-backed wooden chair, well away from the other two women, and took a deep breath. The younger woman, about Clara's age, looked up and smiled.

"Have you been waiting long?" Clara asked. They both looked at their watches.

"My therapist runs a little behind every week," the woman said. "I see Dr. Hathaway."

"This is my first time here,"

The woman smiled. "My name is Mollie."

"Hello. I'm Clara."

"I work here in New Millhaven," Mollie said. "Do you work?"

Clara thought for a moment. "Yes. I'm … I'm a writer."

Mollie's eyes widened. "A real writer? Do you write fiction or nonfiction?"

Clara smiled and was about to tell Mollie about her memoir when a tall, thin woman with a clipboard stepped into the waiting room. "Mrs. Perkins?"

Clara glanced at Mollie. "It was nice to meet you."

Mollie smiled.

Clara followed the woman with the clipboard down a long corridor with yellow walls; on both sides different office doors were identified with metal nameplates. The woman opened the last door on the right and invited Clara into a small office with a large paned window on one wall and two worn overstuffed blue chairs. A small coffee table sat across from a new-looking brown leather recliner; that must be the doctor's chair, Clara thought.

The woman extended her hand. "I'm Susan Morrison."

Clara shook her hand. "Hello, Dr. Morrison."

"Oh, just call me Susan."

She was older, maybe in her late sixties, with curly grey hair that looked as if it needed taming. She wore baggy grey slacks and an untucked peach-colored floral blouse.

"Have a seat," Susan invited.

Clara chose the chair closest to the doctor and immediately sank so far back her feet came off the ground. Quickly she wriggled forward. "Here," Susan said, put this behind you. She handed Clara a small cream-colored pillow.

"Now, what brings you in today, Clara?"

Clara scooted forward until her feet were firmly on the carpet and took a deep breath. "Well, the other day I had a panic attack, at least that's what my doctor said it was. He suggested I talk it over with a therapist."

Dr. Morrison's thick, grey eyebrows went up as she wrote something on the clipboard. "What do you think caused your panic attack?"

Clara clasped her hands together and shifted in the chair. "Well, um, you see, I have just finished writing a memoir."

Dr. Morrison's eyes widened. She flicked a look at Clara and leaned toward her, her lips pursed. "You have written a book?"

"Yes, I have."

Susan stuck her pencil between her teeth. "What did you write about?"

"About my life when I was growing up."

"And what did you say about your life?" Susan bent her head and scribbled something on her clipboard.

Clara cleared her throat. "I just told about what it was like to grow up in a large family that moved every two years."

"Wow," Susan said. "Moving that often must have made it hard to develop friendships."

Clara leaned toward her. "My father was an engineer. He was transferred all over the country for the various oil companies he worked for." She chose her next words carefully. "I made friends easily, but my sister, Miranda, had a very hard time."

She stopped and swallowed.

"Oh?" Susan wrote some more.

Clara sighed. "Miranda was a year older than I was. She was depressed most of her high school years. She would sleep after school and all day on the weekends. I tried to tell my father, but he said never mind about Miranda's problem, that she would be all right."

"And what happened?"

"Miranda graduated and went to college, but within the first year she had to come home because she was more depressed than ever."

"But you were away at college yourself by then, is that right?"

"Yes. I was just sixteen, but I went away to the University of Wisconsin. My Aunt Sarah kept telling my father that Miranda just needed to outgrow her depression, that she didn't need a doctor. Father and Aunt Sarah were against using any kind of medication."

Susan frowned. "What happened to Miranda?" she asked quietly.

Clara took a deep breath. "Well, after she got married, I intervened and insisted that she see a doctor. She was diagnosed with severe depression."

"And your father never suspected how afflicted she was?"

"My father did whatever Aunt Sarah said. All those years it was obvious Miranda had a problem, but I was the youngest and nobody listened to me."

Susan turned over a new page and continued writing. "What did you say about this in your memoir?"

"Just what I told you. But Aunt Sarah is disgusted with me for even writing a memoir. She seems to think I've divulged a huge secret, but she hasn't even read my book!"

"Have you in fact revealed a huge secret?"

Clara shook her head. "No, I don't think so. I certainly never intended to. Aunt Sarah is upset about something she knows nothing about."

"Maybe your aunt is afraid you revealed something that would be damning to her? Or maybe your father?"

Clara opened her mouth to reply when suddenly the doctor picked up a stack of books from a shelf behind her chair and set them on the coffee table. She picked out a slim volume with an orange and black cover and held it up.

"This book had my family upset with me for years."

Clara stared at her. *What does Dr. Morrison's book have to do with me?*

Susan began talking about her book. She giggled and told Clara about her own sister. "She doesn't speak to me because I used real names and events in my memoir." She went on to talk about her brother, how he had been a drug addict and now had problems with alcohol.

Clara squirmed. *Should Dr. Morrison really be telling me these personal things about her own life?*

The doctor's eyebrows moved up and down as she talked on and on. "My mother told me she never loved me because I reminded her of my father, whom she had divorced."

Clara felt sorry for her, and she couldn't help wondering if the doctor had chosen to be a therapist to find answers to her own problems.

Dr. Morrison started to cry. "I was only seven years old when my mother told me that." She wiped away tears.

Clara grew more and more uncomfortable.

"I still want to be close to my family," the doctor wept.

Clara pressed her lips together. *Is this what Dr. Shu had in mind when he sent me to a therapist? This woman has bigger issues than I have. She doesn't know how to fix her own problems, so how can she possibly help me with mine?*

Suddenly the doctor blurted, "Oh, goodness, look at the time! We've gone over the hour."

"What?"

"Of course, since we're just getting to know each other, I won't bill you extra this time."

Clara just looked at her.

"I will see you at the same time next week," Dr. Morrison said. She shook her hand and gave her an appointment card.

When she got to her car, Clara threw the card on the dashboard. Holy Moly! This woman wanted to talk about *her* problems and charge *me* for her time? This is outrageous!

She should cancel that next appointment. She found herself reaching for the phone to call Trey, but shook her head and tossed the phone back into her purse. Trey wouldn't understand; he had never been a fan of psychotherapists.

*   *   *

On Tuesday Clara drove downtown to Boswell's Bookstore to see what memoir covers looked like. Very soon she would have to decide on a cover for her own book. *I can hardly believe I'm doing this. After all these years of never saying anything personal about myself to anyone, I am actually going to publish a memoir about my life!*

She walked into the store and was standing in front of the memoir section when her heart started to race. Then all at once she could scarcely breathe. *Why am I so frightened?*

She walked quickly outside, climbed in her car, and sat quietly, hoping the pounding in her heart would ease up. After half an hour she gave up. She did need to talk to someone about her anxiety, and she guessed she would have to give Dr. Morrison another chance.

Chapter Three

Are You Listening?

That night Trey walked into the kitchen, took one look at Clara, and gave her a big hug. "How was your day?"

"Frustrating. I went to Boswell's to get some ideas for my book cover. I … I got kind of upset."

"Oh? What's the problem?"

"Deciding what to put on a book cover is not as easy as it sounds," Clara said.

"You'll come up with something," he said. "What's the focus of your book, your whole family? Or some special thing that happened when you were growing up?"

Clara's heart started to pound. Why was this so scary? Was it because her life had been so private up until now and she was exposing herself?

Yes, she definitely needed to continue talking to Dr. Morrison.

*   *   *

Wednesday morning, Clara drove back to Susan Morrison's office. Halfway to Merritt Street she sighed and bit her lip. *There is no way I can take Dr. Morrison seriously when she talks on and on about her own book and ignores my anxiety about mine.* Were all therapists like this?

Today the doctor had on tight plaid ankle-length pants, white socks, and tennis shoes. Her blouse was plaid, too, but not the same plaid. Clara stifled a smile.

She took a seat across from the doctor and watched her poise her sharpened pencil over the clipboard on her lap.

"So, Clara, how did your week go?"

Clara drew in a long, slow breath. "I had another panic attack." She told her about the episode in Boswell's Bookstore.

Susan made notes on her clipboard. "Panic about what?"

Clara opened her mouth, but before she could get a word out, Susan grabbed another one of the books stacked on the coffee table. "This volume is called Life Experiences," she announced.

"Oh?" Clara said politely.

"My family vacationed in France every year," Dr. Morrison began. "We would fly to the south of France, to the town of Lyon. Then we would drive up into the Swiss Alps." For the next hour she talked on and on about her experiences in France.

Here she goes again. Clara leaned forward, trying to get a word in.

"The road to Lenzerheide is treacherous," Dr. Morrison continued. "In the wintertime the snow is three to five feet deep."

Clara waited. As the minutes passed she grew more and more uneasy waiting for the doctor to stop. But she kept talking.

"My parents would yell at each other to stay in the middle of the road so we wouldn't end up in a snowdrift."

Clara glanced down at her watch. The hour was almost up. How could she tell the doctor to stop talking and listen to *her?*

Abruptly, Dr. Morrison raised her voice. "Did you know that in some remote areas snow covers the Alps year-round?"

"No," Clara said, "I didn't know that." She looked pointedly at her watch and cleared her throat. Did she have to remind her therapist that *she* was the patient and was supposed to be the one doing most of the talking?

Finally she tapped her watch. "Dr. Morrison," she interrupted. "The hour is getting away from us."

The doctor went on as if she hadn't heard. "You and your husband really should take a trip to the Alps. Did you know you can get altitude sickness up in the mountains? When we went up to St. Moritz, my mother ended up in the hospital. Altitude sickness."

"Dr. Morrison, it's twenty minutes past two. My hour is up."

"Oh," she said. "Yes, I guess it is. I always get caught up in my stories."

When Clara stood up, the doctor wrote out another appointment card. "I think things are moving right along, Clara. I really enjoy listening to you."

Clara snatched the card. She could not believe this woman! Her therapist had spent another entire hour talking about her own life. *She's not even listening to me! I can hardly get a word in edgewise.*

The waiting room was deserted when she left. She walked to her car and threw the appointment card on the dashboard. This was absurd. For the second time, she had ended up listening to Dr. Morrison's life story!

She pulled out of the parking lot and headed back to Boswell's Bookstore to look at more personal memoir book covers.

The bookstore parking lot was jammed. A large sign in the front window announced "Meet Author Thomas Jonesboro," and inside, a short, paunchy man sat at a table, signing books. She moved closer and noticed the title. *Murder in New Millhaven.* She chuckled and picked it up.

The cover showed cornfields under a dark, threatening sky. She picked up eight copies for the family reunion coming up next month and carried them over to the table.

"That's quite a load of books you have there," he commented.

Clara smiled. "It's for a family reunion."

The author stared at her. "You do know it's a murder mystery, right?"

Clara smiled. "I know. I like the title. When my family gets together, something dramatic always happens. Not a murder, of course, but there are always some hard feelings."

When he nodded, she went on. "You know those warm fuzzy feelings you're supposed to get when your family gets together? That doesn't happen when *my* family gets together."

Jonesboro grinned at her, opened one of the books, and inscribed it. "With warm fuzzy feelings for your family reunion."

Clara laughed out loud, and he inscribed the other seven volumes the same way.

She moved on to the memoir section and bumped into a tall, thin woman with shoulder-length brown hair.

"Mollie!" she exclaimed. "How are you?"

"I'm okay. I just need something to read." Her arms were loaded with books.

"Did you meet Thomas Jonesboro at that table over there, signing his books?"

"It looks like he's very successful," Mollie observed. "There's a long line of people waiting to talk to him."

"I bought eight of his mysteries for my family reunion. I love the title, *Murder in New Millhaven*." She opened a copy to show Mollie what he had written.

Mollie laughed. "That's really funny! You know what they say about family ties, don't you? Family ties are the ones that bind and gag you."

Clara nodded and smiled. "What are you looking for?"

"Memoirs. I like memoirs. I like reading about people's lives."

Clara's face grew hot. She started to perspire and tugged her turtleneck away from her chin.

"I just finished a memoir by Elizabeth Taylor," Mollie said. "Did you know she'd been married eight times?"

"Seven times too many, I think," Clara said.

Mollie went on about the lavish lifestyle the actress had lived, then mentioned how tragic her life had been. "No one would ever know these things if she hadn't written about them."

Clara's heart started to pound. When Mollie started talking about the events in other memoirs she had read, Clara had to remind herself to breathe normally.

"You're a writer, aren't you?" Mollie asked suddenly. "What are you writing about?"

Clara swallowed hard. "I'm writing a memoir. About my life when I was growing up."

"Oh, really? What's the title?"

Clara coughed. "I … I don't have a title." She knew what she wanted to call it, though. Little Girl in Red Shoes.

"I want to read it when it's published," Mollie said.

Clara blinked. Dear God in heaven, when her memoir was in print anybody could read it. People she'd never met would know all about her life, all about her thoughts, her feelings, everything she had kept private all these years. Why had she never considered this before?

Hurriedly she said goodbye, left the bookstore, and climbed into her car. *What did I expect when I started to write a memoir?* She wondered now why she'd ever thought that writing about her life was a good idea.

When she got home, Trey gave her a hug. "What's for dinner? I've had a really stressful day."

He'd had a stressful day! What about her? With a sigh she went to the refrigerator and was just pulling out some steaks when the phone rang. Oh, God, it was Aunt Sarah.

"Clara?" Her aunt's voice sounded tense. "I need you to help me tomorrow."

"Help you with what?"

"Well ..." Aunt Sarah hesitated. "I've been working in the basement, organizing some old photographs. But the boxes are too heavy for me to lift, so could you—?"

"Sure, Aunt Sarah. I'll come over tomorrow morning."

She hung up the receiver, but the more she thought about it, the odder her aunt's request seemed. Aunt Sarah had never let anyone in her basement. Why now?

* * *

That night Clara woke with a jolt and sat up in bed. Her heart raced and she was sweating. *What is happening to me?*

Quietly she got up and walked down the hallway to the kitchen. While she sipped a glass of water she tried to remember what she'd been dreaming about before she woke up. All at once it came back to her.

Aunt Sarah was hovering over her, pointing her finger and shouting, "Stop, Clara! Stop!"

Chapter Four

Helping Aunt Sarah

Clara dressed in jeans and an untucked white blouse and left the house at nine the next morning. Something nagged at her. Something to do with her memoir. Had she left something out? What about the ending? Maybe no one would care about her life story.

Aunt Sarah lived on St. Francis Drive in a charming three-story house white house with green shutters, neatly groomed flower beds, and a curved brick walkway. Clara knew her aunt's basement was crammed with odds and ends she had accumulated over her 87 years, but she had never been allowed down there.

She rang the doorbell and from somewhere inside the house heard her aunt's voice. "Come on in, Clara."

She let herself in and glanced around at the unusually cluttered living room.

"I'm down here in the basement, Clara. Come on down."

She blinked in disbelief. She was actually being invited into Aunt Sarah's inner sanctum?

The stairs creaked as she descended, and she wrinkled her nose at the sharp smell in the chilly air. When she reached the concrete floor she saw her aunt in the far corner, sitting on an old stool next to a stack of cardboard boxes.

"Aunt Sarah, what are you doing down here?"

"Clara, come here and look at these photographs. I have things on my mind, and at my age I might not have much time left to talk about them."

"Oh, Aunt Sarah, you always say that." Still, she could never remember her aunt looking so old and frail.

Aunt Sarah put a photograph in Clara's hand. "This is when your mother and I were little girls."

Clara stared at it. The picture showed two chubby little blonde girls, one with very curly hair, the other with a straight bob and bangs.

"Clara, you look a lot like your mother."

"I don't remember her very clearly, Aunt Sarah. After Mama died, you were like my mother."

Her aunt had a faraway smile on her wrinkled face. "Your mother had dreams. We talked about those dreams over the years, and when your mother met your father, one of her dreams came true."

Clara smoothed one finger over the photo until her aunt slipped it back into a thick black album. "Now, I want you to see some more." They sorted through two boxes of scrapbooks and photograph albums, but when Clara reached for the next box on the stack, Aunt Sarah slapped her hand away.

"No! Don't touch that box!"

"But Aunt Sarah …"

"No buts," she snapped. "Leave that alone."

"All right, all right, I won't open that box."

"It's time for lunch anyway," her aunt said. "Let's go upstairs. I've made sandwiches."

Clara helped her up the stairs, wondering how much longer her aunt would be able to get down to her basement.

Upstairs in the neat, all-white kitchen, her aunt slipped a photo of Clara and her sister, Miranda, out of her apron pocket. "Just look at you two. You and Miranda look just like your mother and me."

Clara nodded. She and Miranda had always been close, just as Aunt Sarah and their mother had been.

They ate tuna sandwiches and sliced tomatoes and talked about the photos until Aunt Sarah suddenly stopped eating and laid her hand on Clara's. "You know, Clara, your mother would not like it if you wrote certain things about the family."

"What things? What are you talking about?"

Her aunt dropped her head into her hands. "Clara, you can't write about your life, about the family and everything. You just can't."

Clara stared at her. "But Aunt Sarah, I've already written my memoir. It's about to be published. What is it you're so worried about?"

"I am quite sure you know what I'm talking about."

"No, I don't. Aunt Sarah, this doesn't make any sense. You haven't even read my memoir!"

"No, I haven't. And I don't want to."

Clara caught her breath. "Why not? What are you afraid of?"

Her aunt's face changed. "Nothing," she said quickly. "I'm not afraid of anything."

"Then what is your objection to—"

"You simply can't put private things, secrets about our family, out for the whole world to see."

"But—"

"I'm tired now. You need to go home, child."

Clara slowly stood up. She had never seen her aunt look so old. Or so angry. What on earth was she talking about? What secrets?

Chapter Five

The Real Question

That night over dinner Clara told Trey about her dissatisfaction with Dr. Morrison.

Trey frowned. "Will you be charged for those sessions where she did all the talking?"

"I don't know," she sighed. "Maybe I've learned a lesson."

He frowned. "Honey, what's really bothering you?"

She was silent for a long minute. "Trey, if I knew the answer to that, I wouldn't need to see a therapist."

"Yeah, I guess not." After dessert he settled into his favorite chair and fell asleep, leaving Clara feeling upset and dissatisfied. She glanced over at him in his recliner. She knew her husband didn't put much stock in professional counseling, but she wanted him to understand her frustration.

She walked into the kitchen and stared at the dinner dishes waiting in the sink. She felt tired and confused and alone. She couldn't think about Aunt Sarah or her book or Trey any longer;

instead she decided get her mind off everything and do something useful, like wash the dishes.

She had just picked up a plate when the phone rang. "Clara?"

She caught her breath. It was Aunt Sarah again.

"Clara, I want you to come over."

"Now?" Clara blurted.

"It won't take long. I've been working in the basement, and I need you to carry a heavy box upstairs for me."

"Now, really? Can't it wait until tomorrow?"

"No, it can't."

Clara untied her apron, left a note for Trey, and climbed into the Volvo. On the drive over she felt increasingly apprehensive. Aunt Sarah had acted … strange when she'd been helping her earlier.

When she arrived, her aunt was waving to her from the front porch. "There you are! I thought you'd forgotten."

"Aunt Sarah, what is so important that it couldn't wait until tomorrow?"

Her aunt didn't answer. Clara followed her into the house, and when she closed the front door, Aunt Sarah turned to her. "I need you to come down to the basement with me."

She hesitated. "Why don't you just tell me which box you want moved and I'll bring it up?"

"No," her aunt snapped. "I don't want you rummaging around on your own down there."

Clara blinked. She took her aunt's bony arm and very slowly they made their way down the dimly lit stairwell. When they reached the bottom, Aunt Sarah pointed across the floor. "Don't go over there."

"Why not?" Now she saw that all the boxes had been re-stacked. "Where are the boxes we looked through before?"

"Never you mind," her aunt said.

There were marks on the dusty floor where something had apparently been dragged across it. Clara tried to see where the marks ended.

"That's the box I need taken upstairs," Aunt Sarah announced, pointing to a large cardboard carton. "It is too heavy for me to carry, but I need it in the living room."

The box was marked Personal and Private. Clara tried to lift it into her arms, but it was too bulky. She dragged it across to the stairs and then very carefully she managed to heft it up the stairs, one step at a time. When she reached the kitchen, Aunt Sarah was waiting.

"Be careful with that, Clara! Put it next to my rocking chair."

She pushed it across the living room floor to her aunt's old walnut rocker, then sat down to catch her breath.

But Aunt Sarah had other ideas. "Have you decided not to publish that memoir?" she asked with narrowed eyes.

The question surprised her. "No, I haven't."

"Clara, what I'm asking is important. And don't think I'm being a crotchety old lady. Just because I'm old doesn't mean I'm senile."

"Aunt Sarah, your age has nothing to do with my book. Why don't you tell me why you feel I shouldn't publish it."

Her aunt sank down in the rocker and stared at the unopened box, her veined hands clasped in her lap. "You do care about your family, don't you?"

"Of course I care about them."

"Well," her aunt said, leaning forward and peering into her face. "That should be reason enough."

Exasperated, Clara propped her hands on her hips. "What on earth does that mean? Nothing you say makes any sense, Aunt Sarah. And since you haven't read my memoir, I'm going to bring over the manuscript pages so you can. Then maybe you can show me exactly what you are so worried about."

"Don't you dare bring that book into my house!"

"What? That's ridiculous. If you won't even look at it, I have no way of knowing what your objection is about."

Her aunt just looked at her but said nothing.

"I'm going home now, Aunt Sarah." Shaking, she walked through the front door and out onto the porch. By the time she reached her car, her pulse was racing.

She stewed about it all the way home. The whole thing made no sense. When she walked into the living room, she told Trey everything that had happened.

"Leave it alone, Clara. Your aunt is an old woman, set in her ways and narrow-minded. She's got some bee in her bonnet about something, but if I were you, I'd just ignore it. And her."

Clara sighed. "That doesn't help much," she said.

"Maybe it doesn't, honey. But I think you and Aunt Sarah will just have to agree to disagree. And when you see her, don't talk about your memoir."

Right at this moment it felt as if her husband didn't want to be bothered with the problem. "Trey, do you think Aunt Sarah is right? Maybe what a person writes about one's family should always remain private?"

"Don't put me in the middle of this, Clara. Just make sure you didn't reveal anything detrimental about your family."

"But that's just it! I don't think I wrote anything very revealing, but apparently Aunt Sarah does!"

Trey gave her an odd look. "Do you want me to read your book?"

Clara hesitated. "Okay," she said slowly. Then all at once she got a really uneasy feeling and changed her mind. "No," she said decisively. "It's *my* book, about me and my family when I was growing up. I don't want anyone to read it until it's published. Even you."

He shrugged. "Well, all right, I guess. Just don't expect me to be sympathetic when Aunt Sarah gives you a hard time."

Clara's mouth tightened. He could at least say that he was on her side, that he understood how important it was to her that she'd actually written a book.

That night she lay awake for hours. Regardless of Aunt Sarah's objections, the more she thought about putting her thoughts and feelings about her family, all the things she remembered about growing up, out there for the entire world to read about, the more uneasy she grew. She had always kept things to herself, never talked about herself or her life before she and Trey were married and raised their children. Now in a very real way it felt like she was "coming out of the closet."

Suddenly the whole idea of publishing her memoir was really scary, and it had nothing, absolutely nothing, to do with Aunt Sarah. Maybe she shouldn't do it?

*   *   *

The next afternoon Clara had another appointment with Dr. Morrison. As usual, the doctor appeared with her clipboard and ushered her past the white-noise machines in the hallway to her office. When she entered, she saw that another of Dr. Morrison's books lay on the coffee table. This one was titled *My Journey*. Clara sighed.

"How have you been since our last appointment?" the doctor asked.

"Really busy," Clara replied. "I've been reading over my manuscript for the last time before sending it to the publisher." She opened her mouth to tell her about Aunt Sarah's basement and the box of photographs when Dr. Morrison suddenly cleared her throat.

"Did you buy a copy of my book?" she asked. "Have you read it yet?"

Clara frowned. "No, I haven't. As I said, I've had a really busy week working on my own book."

The doctor wrote something on the clipboard. "We all have a journey to walk in life," she said. She reached for *My Journey*, opened it to a page in the middle, and started to read aloud.

Clara squirmed, but the doctor just continued reading. She didn't even look up.

Ten minutes passed. "Um, Dr. Morrison? Shouldn't I be the one doing the talking?"

The doctor glanced up, her eyebrows lifting. "Why, Clara, if you would do your homework, I wouldn't need to hear exactly what is on your mind."

"Excuse me? What homework? Dr. Morrison, I feel as if you're treating me like a child."

The doctor sat up straight. "Is that what you think?"

Clara drew in a long, slow breath. "Yes, that is what I think. I am here to talk about my anxiety, but you keep talking about your books. I'm afraid this is not working out."

"But Clara, we are making such progress!"

"No, we aren't. How can you say that when you're doing all the talking instead of listening to me?" She stood up. "I think this is our last session."

She shook the doctor's hand, then turned away and walked quickly down the hallway. Mollie was sitting in the waiting room, and Clara sat down beside her. "Mollie," do you mind if I ask you something?"

"No, I don't mind at all. Go ahead."

Clara lowered her voice. "Does your therapist mostly talk about himself during a session?"

"Oh, no. I do all the talking, and he listens."

Clara thought for a moment. "My therapist is a writer. She talks on and on about her books, and she did it again today. She even read out loud from one of them!"

"That seems odd," Mollie said.

"I think so, too, and I'm not coming back. I'm going to call my doctor and get another recommendation." She felt so relieved at her decision she decided to re-visit Boswell's Bookstore and check out more book covers.

In the memoir section she found covers featuring photographs of people, landscapes, even books with only the title and the author's name. Nothing seemed quite right for her memoir cover, but she had to decide on something before it went to press.

Then she pulled out a book that made her catch her breath. On the cover was the silhouette of a woman against a dark blue sky;

looking at it made her nervous for some reason. Why on earth would this bother her?

She re-shelved it and selected another. This one showed an adorable little girl on the cover. She turned it over and read the blurb on the back. "A study of children from dysfunctional families."

The child looked perfectly normal, but Clara knew that on the outside a person might not show the inner trauma they had experienced. Suddenly she felt like crying.

She shoved the book back into its space and quickly left the bookstore. When she reached her car, she found her cell phone and dialed Dr. Shu. The receptionist put her through right away.

"Clara!" Dr. Shu said. "What's wrong?"

She swallowed. "You know I have been seeing Dr. Susan Morrison, as you suggested."

"Yes. How is that working out for you?"

"It's not working out at all. I need to talk about the anxiety I'm feeling, but I'm really puzzled about the sessions. Dr. Morrison talks more about her own life and the books she's written and her own experiences than about my feelings."

"You mean to tell me she is talking about herself? In your therapy sessions?"

"Yes. That's mostly all she does." Clara covered her eyes with her hand. "Dr. Shu, could you please recommend someone else?"

Chapter Six

New Beginning

The following morning Clara's cell phone rang.

"Mrs. Perkins? This is Dr. Renée Craig. I am a psychotherapist. Dr. Arthur Shu asked me to call you."

Clara's heart skipped a beat.

"Mrs. Perkins," the soft low voice asked, "can you tell me the general reason why you are seeking counseling?"

Clara cleared her throat. "I am having anxiety attacks. Dr. Shu calls them panic attacks. I'd never had them before, and he thinks I should talk to someone about them."

"I see. Have you any idea what is causing them?"

Oh, God. Should I tell Dr. Craig about my memoir? "Um, well, I've written a book. It's a memoir, actually. But now that I'm about to publish it, I'm starting to feel really uneasy."

"Is there a problem about publishing it?"

Clara took a deep breath. "Well, yes, there is. My aunt disapproves of my writing something that is personally revealing, and lately I've started to feel really frightened about it. Does that make sense?"

"It makes perfect sense. Could you bring a copy of the manuscript over to my office today?"

For a moment she couldn't think. "I guess so. Do you really think reading it will be helpful?"

"I do, yes. I will take very good care of it."

"All right. I'll make a copy and bring it over." She jotted down the address, then gathered up the manuscript pages and started off for Copy and Go. On the way, she decided to make two copies, one for Dr. Craig, and one for Trey. If a stranger was going to read her story, Trey should read it, too.

What if Dr. Craig doesn't like what I wrote? Worse, what if Trey doesn't like it? What if he finds something I shouldn't have written about?

She sat in the Copy and Go parking lot with music blaring on the car radio, trying to work up her courage. *Get out of the car, Clara. You know what you need to do.*

Inside, a short woman wearing a brown apron was standing behind the counter. "May I help you?"

Clara bit her lip. "I need two copies of this manuscript. I'll wait for them."

"No problem," the clerk said.

She handed over her manuscript pages and watched the woman walk across the room to a large machine, stopping to speak to a coworker. Then she placed the pages neatly in the machine and walked away.

Where is she going?

The clerk came back to slide some paper into the copy machine, still talking to her coworker across the room. Then the machine began spitting out pages. Suddenly it stopped. The clerk grabbed the two stacks of pages and loaded them and the original manuscript into two Copy and Go cardboard boxes.

"You're all set," she said.

Outside, Clara carefully placed the manuscripts on the back seat of her Volvo and drove straight to the address Dr. Craig had given her.

The doctor's office turned out to be an older two-story house, brown with beige trim, and neatly landscaped with blooming chrysanthemums along the steep driveway and pots of yellow daisies by the front door. A sign stuck in one pot read, "Please wait patiently."

She rang the doorbell and waited. After a few minutes, someone inside yelled, "Just a minute!" Then the front door opened and a petite woman in her sixties with short, curly, jet black hair smiled at her. She wore a pink jogging outfit.

"I'm Dr. Craig. May I help you?"

"I'm Clara Perkins. I brought you my manuscript."

"Ah, this is the book you've written?"

Clara nodded, and the doctor reached for the box Clara clutched to her chest. "I'll have this back to you at your appointment on Friday."

"Okay." She felt really uneasy about leaving it, but she tried to smile. The door closed, and she walked out to the driveway and climbed into her car. Suddenly there was Dr. Craig, tapping on her windshield.

"Clara, when you come on Friday, please park on the street."

That seemed like an odd request when the doctor had a perfectly good driveway, but Clara nodded, started the Volvo, and drove away.

*   *   *

On Friday Clara put on navy blue trousers and a loose, cream-colored silk blouse. By the time she'd applied some pale rose lipstick, her nerves were on edge.

She turned into the driveway on David Lane and had just started to get out of her car when Dr. Craig came running up. Her face was flushed.

"I said to park on the street!"

"Oh, I'm sorry. I forgot." Quickly she re-started the Volvo, backed down the driveway, and parked in front of the house. Dr. Craig was waiting for her at the front door.

"Hello there!" The doctor smiled.

"Hi," Clara said. She was a bit out of breath from climbing up the steep driveway. Dr. Craig invited her inside.

The entryway had grey and white marble tile. To the right was a living room with a worn blue sofa covered in a floral pattern and an old oval maple coffee table. Two overstuffed chairs flanked the sofa, and a huge oil seascape hung over the sofa. A blue sheet covered the doorway into another room.

"Please have a seat and I'll have you fill out some paperwork." She handed Clara a clipboard and a pen and disappeared.

Clara took one of the overstuffed chairs, filled out the paperwork, and waited. And waited. Finally, after many minutes, Dr. Craig walked back into the room and ushered her down the hallway to her office.

"Take a chair in the corner over there." She pointed to two black leather chairs. A glass table sat between them with a box of Kleenex on top.

Dr. Craig settled in the other black chair, a scant three feet away from her. Clara noticed her desk was overflowing with a jumble of books and papers. Through the partially open window she could hear the sound of a waterfall.

"First of all," Dr. Craig began, "please call me Renée."

Clara nodded.

"Well," the doctor continued, "how are you feeling today?"

"Fine," Clara lied. Her nerves felt as if an electric current was running through them.

Dr. Craig gave her a long look. "Clara, I have to say that you have written an unusual book."

Clara sat up straighter and clasped her hands tight in her lap. "You read it all?" She could scarcely breathe. *What did she think of it?*

"Of course I read it! Now, tell me, what made you want to write about your life?"

Clara leaned forward. "Well, now that my children are grown and gone, I find I have time on my hands. I started to think back about my own family when I was growing up and—" All at once she sneezed.

"Were you thinking about anything in particular?"

"My family was quite large, and we moved all over the country. I had an interesting childhood." She sneezed again and her eyes started to water. She snatched a Kleenex out of the box and blotted them.

"How long did it take you to write your story?" the doctor asked.

"From start to finish, it took me almost a year." She sneezed again.

"Wow! That was fast! Do you have an agent?"

Clara sat back in her chair. "An agent? No, I—" She sneezed again. "I apologize. I must be allergic to something."

Dr. Craig pursed her lips. "Your Aunt Sarah is a real character. And all those siblings! It's a wonder your father could keep up with all of you after your mother died."

Clara sighed. "I don't remember much about my mother."

"Um-hmmm. Tell me, what do your siblings think about your book?"

Clara wiped her eyes and sneezed again.

"You must have a severe allergy," Dr. Craig said.

"Yes, I'm highly allergic to cats.

"Oh, I have a cat. But she's strictly an outdoor cat. Do you like cats?"

Clara sneezed again. She didn't want to talk about cats. She wanted to talk about her anxiety. "Dr. Craig, I need to tell you about the stress I'm feeling about my memoir."

"Oh, you already have," the doctor replied.

"I have?"

Dr. Craig paid no attention. "You know, I wrote a book myself three years ago. It's called *Lifestrings*. I tried to get a publisher, but it was difficult. Are you having any luck?"

Clara gritted her teeth. Oh, no, not another session with a therapist talking about her own book. *Give me a break!* Her eyes were watering, so she pulled out another Kleenex and dabbed at the moisture.

"I love how you pulled me into your story," the doctor went on. "I felt like I was watching you grow up. In my own book, I talk about my family, too. My parents didn't move around like yours did, but I also came from a large family."

Clara blotted at her watery eyes. "Are you sure your cat stays outside?"

"Of course I'm sure. Why?"

"I'm really allergic to cats."

The doctor just laughed and went on as if she hadn't heard. "That part when you were traveling across the country and one of your siblings was accidentally left at a grocery store was really funny!"

Clara tried to smile and sneaked a look at her watch. Dr. Craig had talked about her own book for 20 minutes! And she hadn't asked a single question about Clara's panic attacks.

"Are you going to write another book?" the doctor asked. "Maybe a sequel?"

Clara drew in an extra-long breath. "The first thing I have to do is get over my anxiety attacks," she said. "That is why I am here."

She didn't know if she was angry because Dr. Craig kept talking about herself or because there was obviously a cat that was most definitely *not* outdoors but somewhere inside the house.

"Excuse me, Dr. Craig, but I'm having a real problem being here. Your cat may be an outdoor cat, but my allergic reaction is getting worse and worse."

"Oh, no, it can't be my cat. I told you my cat is an outside cat!"

Clara blew her nose one last time and stood up. "That may be, but—"

"Wait!" the doctor said. "My book, *Lifestrings*, is about different stages we all go through during the course of our lives."

Clara just looked at her.

"Now, I'm turning sixty-five this week. That's a hard birthday to take, but I know about different stages in life. I know I should have waited awhile to finish my book, but the last few years have been extremely revealing to me because I've sort of come into my own. So I wanted to share my experiences with others. You understand?"

Clara pressed her lips together. *Oh, I understand all right. I understand that you think your life experiences are more important than mine. But I am the patient here. I am paying you to help me!*

That afternoon when Clara drove home she couldn't wait to get to her medicine cabinet and grab some antihistamine. Her eyes felt puffy and her nose was running. She lay down for an hour, then got up and went into the kitchen for some iced tea.

That evening over spaghetti, Trey asked about her appointment with Dr. Craig.

Clara laid her fork on her dinner plate. "She works out of her home. And she has a cat!" she blurted.

Trey looked at her from across the dining table and shook his head. "Honey, didn't you tell her you're allergic to cats?"

"Yes, I did. But she insisted it was an outdoor cat! I couldn't stop sneezing and my eyes were watering I … it was awful. Not only that, she didn't ask about my anxiety at all. She just talked about herself."

Her husband's eyebrows went up. "Let me get this straight. The first therapist you saw talked about her own books and charged you for the time, and this one has a cat and ignored the fact that you told her that you're allergic?"

"Well, yes." She couldn't bring herself to tell him Dr. Craig was another writer who'd also published a book. "It sounds crazy, doesn't it?"

"Sure does."

"Now I'm beginning to have even more anxiety. Maybe I shouldn't publish my memoir."

"You don't really mean that, do you?" He got up and came around the table to hug her. "This will all work out, honey."

"Not if I can't handle my anxiety."

Trey patted her shoulder. "You will handle it, eventually."

She opened her mouth to tell him how discouraged she was feeling, but he disappeared into the living room and settled into his favorite chair. She started to clear the plates away and noticed he had fallen asleep.

How can he do that, just fall asleep in the middle of a conversation?

She was beginning to feel overwhelmed. She needed someone to *talk* to!

The phone rang. Oh no, not Aunt Sarah again. She was distracted enough.

"It's Mollie," the woman said. "How about meeting for coffee tomorrow?"

Oh, what a relief, someone to talk to!

In the morning, when Trey left for his golf game, Clara drove over to The Tea Leaf to meet Mollie. She was sitting in the window, waving, as she walked in the door. "Clara! How are you?"

Tears stung her eyes. "Awful," she choked out.

Mollie reached across the table to grasp her hand. "What on earth is wrong?"

Clara sighed. "I had no idea my memoir would be such a problem. Not writing it. It's publishing it that's the problem. My Aunt Sarah thinks I've written about something I shouldn't have, but she won't tell me what it is. She won't even read the manuscript!"

"That is frustrating," Mollie said. "And unfair."

"Honestly, I just wrote about things I think everyone experiences when they are growing up. I keep re-reading my manuscript trying to figure out what Aunt Sarah could possibly object to, but I can't find anything. Nothing. I'm starting to have nightmares about it."

"You're seeing a new therapist, aren't you? Is that helping?"

Clara groaned. "Don't I wish! This new person, Dr. Craig, asked to read the manuscript, and she said she loved what I'd written. But then she talked on and on for the whole hour about the book *she* had written!"

"You mean she didn't ask about your anxiety or your nightmares?"

"No. And this is what I don't understand, Mollie. This is the second therapist who has spent my entire appointment hour talking about herself."

Mollie stared at her. "That's really weird."

"My aunt is furious with me. I'm not sleeping at night, and I've been to two therapists and neither of them was helpful. I don't know what to do next."

"Let me give you the name of my brother's therapist. His name is Dr. Timothy Stevens. Maybe male doctors are more responsive. And maybe," Mollie added with a laugh, "he hasn't written any books!"

Clara dug in her purse for a pen.

Chapter Seven

Dinner, Anyone?

Trey and Clara were getting ready to leave for Miranda's house to have dinner when the phone rang. "Clara?" her sister said. "Could you pick up Aunt Sarah on your way over? I'd do it, but I burned my piecrust and I have to make another one."

"Sure," Clara said.

"Oh, and Clara? Do you know why Aunt Sarah is so upset with you? She spent the better part of this afternoon telling me what a bad apple you are."

Clara blinked. "What did she say?"

"Something about what she wants you to do that you won't do." Miranda laughed. "I think it's something about that book you wrote."

Clara said nothing. She didn't find it funny at all. "What on earth did you write about?" Miranda asked.

"It's really just about when we were growing up, how we moved around so much and the funny things that happened in our family when we were young."

"Aunt Sarah thinks you've divulged a huge family secret."

"Well, it must be something only Aunt Sarah knows about, because I sure don't know what it is." She hung up the phone and began to pace around the kitchen.

"What was all that about?" Trey asked.

"Aunt Sarah is telling Miranda all about how mad at me she is."

"What do you care?"

"I care because I'm having anxiety attacks!" she snapped. "Haven't you been listening?"

"Well, sure, honey. You know I always listen to you." He helped her on with her coat. "Come on, let's go pick up your crazy aunt."

*   *   *

When Aunt Sarah answered her front door and found Trey standing there she gave him a puzzled look. "What are you doing here?"

He bent to kiss her cheek. "Miranda burned her piecrust, and she's making another one, so we're picking you up tonight," he said with a smile. He helped her into the Volvo and reached over to buckle her seatbelt, but she slapped his hand away. "I can do that myself."

Trey gave Clara a sideways look and raised his eyebrows.

They drove to Miranda's house in silence.

*   *   *

Miranda, Clara's older sister by only a year, was the one who hosted all the family dinners. She lived on the other side of town in a well-kept two-story house with white trim. An evergreen Christmas wreath hung on the front door.

When the door opened Aunt Sarah pushed her way past Clara, calling for Miranda. Clara followed her into the kitchen where the family members were standing around and watched her aunt make a beeline for her sister.

The room went quiet and Trey reached for Clara's hand. "Are you going to talk about your memoir tonight?" he asked in an undertone.

Clara's heart skipped a beat. "Not if I can help it."

"Will you let me read it?"

"Yes. When I made a copy for Dr. Craig, I made one for you, too."

"That's the counselor with the cat?"

She rolled her eyes. "Yes, the counselor with the cat."

"Are you going back to her again?" he murmured.

Her heart raced just thinking about it. "No, I'm not."

She stood in the kitchen doorway, trying to hear what Miranda and Aunt Sarah were whispering about. Her aunt was gesturing with a pointed forefinger, and her sister was frowning and shaking her head. When Aunt Sarah caught sight of Clara, she stopped talking.

Clara's palms began to sweat. It was obvious something was going on. "Hi, Miranda," she said in the most normal voice she could manage.

Miranda hugged her. She was wearing a black suit with a red satin blouse underneath, and her hair was pulled up in a neat bun. "Clara, what's new?"

"Nothing much."

"That's not true," her aunt said. "Your sister has written the most awful book!" she said loudly.

Aunt Sarah's two brothers, Uncle Joe and Uncle Larry, stared at her. Joe was stout, with a full head of grey hair. Larry was younger, tall, and well-built, with a dark mustache.

Clara's heart felt ready to jump out of her chest. She escaped into the living room where her sister Casey and her husband, Jerry, sat on the cream-colored sofa. Short, plump Casey was the oldest. She was always behind the times in fashion, and tonight she wore a loose denim jumper with a purple blouse and black slip-on shoes with long knit stockings.

"Everyone take a seat in the dining room," Miranda called. "Dinner is ready."

Clara motioned for Trey to sit next to her at the table, and when he took his chair, he squeezed her hand.

"Don't mention my book," she whispered.

Casey and Jerry, who never said anything if he could help it, sat across from them. "Miranda says Clara's written a book about our family," Casey announced. "About our childhood."

"And," Aunt Sarah added, "she's going to publish it!"

"What is so interesting about our childhood, Clara?" her sister inquired in her booming, take-charge voice. Casey was known in the family as "the enforcer"; it was her way or no way at all.

"I guess we'll have to read it and find out, Uncle Larry said, pulling on his suspenders.

"It's not published yet," Clara said quickly.

"Yeah? When will that be?"

"Not soon enough," Miranda joked.

"I want to know what she says about us," Uncle Joe boomed. "Trey, have you read it?"

"No, I haven't, Joe."

Clara swallowed hard. She should never have told anyone what she was writing about.

"Pass my plate to Miranda to fill," Aunt Sarah announced. While they passed the plate from hand to hand, her aunt looked right at her, her eyes narrowed. Then she leaned close to Casey and started to whisper.

Uncle Larry leaned in from the other side and murmured something under his breath.

"We'll just ask her," Casey blurted.

Clara groaned inwardly.

Her sister was sitting between Uncle Larry and Uncle Joe, a stout, feisty man in his eighties. He always had a smile on his face, but tonight Aunt Sarah was whispering something to him and his forehead creased into a frown.

What are they whispering about?

Casey leaned forward and cleared her throat. "Clara? What's this I hear about you writing a book?"

Clara swallowed. "Yes, it's a memoir, about when we were growing up."

"How dare you write about us without telling us!" Casey snapped. Her face was tight with disapproval. Casey thought she was right all the time and told everyone so.

Trey pressed Clara's hand. "I think it's great," he said. "The kids are gone and Clara's found something interesting to do in her free time."

Miranda gave him a quizzical look. "What free time? Seems to me Clara is kept pretty busy cooking all the meals and keeping your house clean."

Trey said nothing.

"When were you going to tell us about your book, Clara?" Casey inquired, her voice accusing.

"It's no secret. I thought you all knew I've been doing some writing."

Casey glared at her. "So, are you exposing us?"

"Exposing you? Of course not. It's not that kind of book, Casey. I would never write about my family in a negative way."

Uncle Joe frowned. "Then we all want copies to read, don't we? And, young lady, we'll let you know if you can publish this thing or not!"

Clara caught her breath. "If I can publish … Uncle Joe, I feel that decision rests with me, as the author. Not you or anyone else."

"Not good enough," Uncle Joe growled.

Clara gritted her teeth. "You can all read it when it's published," she said quietly.

Uncle Larry whispered something to Aunt Sarah, who frowned. "I don't know if that's in the book," she murmured. He crossed his arms and tipped his chair back.

This is ridiculous! I offered to let Aunt Sarah read it, but she refused. What is everyone's problem?

She excused herself and went down the hall into the bathroom and locked the door. Her heart was pounding, and in the mirror she saw that her face and neck were flaming. She dipped a face towel in cold water and patted her cheeks. Her hands shook.

"Why are they being so negative?" she muttered. "My memoir is nobody's business but mine!"

After a long ten minutes she took a deep breath and walked back into the dining room. Aunt Sarah and Uncle Larry were shouting at Trey. He stood up and pulled out her chair for her.

"What took you so long?" he breathed. "The wolves are out tonight."

She just looked at him.

"Why are you being so secretive about your book?" Casey demanded.

"Secretive! I'm not being secretive about it! It was no secret that I've been writing a book."

Casey rolled her eyes and reached over to pat Aunt Sarah's hand. "It's going to be all right," she said in an undertone.

Clara's spine stiffened. "What's going to be all right?" she asked. "What do you think I wrote about?"

The entire table fell silent.

"I've finished my dinner," Aunt Sarah announced. "I want to go home now."

"But Clara hasn't eaten a bite yet," Trey objected.

Nevertheless, Aunt Sarah pushed her chair back from the table and both Uncle Joe and a scowling Uncle Larry stood up and followed her to the living room.

Clara stared at her plate, but she couldn't bring herself to pick up her fork. "I have no appetite, Trey. Let's just take Aunt Sarah home." She carried both their plates into the kitchen.

Casey and Miranda stood at the sink, whispering. "Clara," Casey called, "what's the title of your book?"

Clara set the plates in the sink. "*Little Girl in Red Shoes.*"

"Huh!" she exclaimed. "What do red shoes have to do with us?"

"Glory be to God," Aunt Sarah shouted from the living room, "she's going to tell everything!"

Clara left the kitchen and stepped into the living room. "What 'everything', Aunt Sarah? What are you talking about?"

Aunt Sarah turned her back and muttered something under her breath to her brothers. Uncle Larry patted his sister's shoulder, but she was not smiling.

Clara fled back to the kitchen where Miranda stood at the sink, starting to wash dishes. "Miranda, when I decide on the book cover, I'll give you a copy of the manuscript to read."

"Oh, Clara, thanks. I'm sure I will love your memoir."

Clara tried to smile. "Why is everyone else so upset about it?"

Miranda shrugged. "Beats me."

Clara hugged her sister and went to find Trey. Aunt Sarah was already heading for the front door with her purse on her arm. She kissed Casey and Jerry, but Clara was pointedly ignored. Stunned, she stared at her family. *What was going on?*

After a short drive, Trey parked the Volvo and walked Aunt Sarah up to her front door. Just before she stepped inside she stretched up and whispered something in his ear.

When he got back in the car, Clara leaned over and asked, "What was all that about?"

"Same old thing, honey. She doesn't want you to publish your memoir."

She sighed. "I have a copy of the manuscript for you in the back seat if you'd like you to read it." She reached back for the Copy and Go box with her pages, but it was gone.

"Trey, I left the manuscript on the back seat, but it's not there. Did you take it?"

"Oh, I forgot to tell you. Before we picked everybody up, I locked your manuscript in the trunk."

"My nerves are really on edge, I guess."

Trey looked over at her. "I'm sure not picking up on what your aunt is so worried about." When they got home he unlocked the trunk and handed the manuscript box to her. She checked to make sure all the pages were there and laid it in his hands. It felt as if she were giving him a piece of her heart.

Once inside the house, Clara walked into her office to check her emails; one was from the cover artist, asking when she should expect the final decision about the book cover. She typed her response and pressed Send.

In the family room she found her husband in his recliner, reading her manuscript with a red pencil in his hand. Her heart skipped a beat. She moved closer.

"Trey? What are you doing?"

He didn't look up. "Reading your book." He jotted something in the margin on one page and crossed out a paragraph.

"You're marking up my manuscript?" She couldn't keep the hurt from her voice.

"I'm just making a note here and there," he said.

She stifled the impulse to snatch back the pages. Instead, she decided to go on to bed and talk about it in the morning.

Somewhere around 4 o'clock Trey climbed into bed and fell instantly asleep while she lay staring up at the ceiling.

The next morning she rose very early and walked into the kitchen. Her manuscript sat on the kitchen counter with Trey's red pencil on top, so she lifted the title page and began to read his notes.

She was unprepared for the shock. He had marked out entire paragraphs! Important paragraphs, filled with all her feelings about being the youngest child in a large family. He hated her memoir!

Stunned, she curled up on the living room sofa and sipped coffee until Trey woke up. It was Saturday morning so she knew he didn't have to go to work. She read for the next two hours and by the time he appeared, she had worked herself into an emotional meltdown.

When he walked in, she was crying.

Instantly he looked concerned. "Honey, what's wrong?"

She held up her manuscript. "You didn't like my memoir," she wept.

He sat down beside her. "Oh, sweetie, that's not true. I loved your book! I mean it. I couldn't put it down."

"Then w-why did you mark it all up?"

"Oh, I don't know. I guess I'm not as emotional as you are. I wouldn't have revealed so much of my feelings." He put his arms around her.

She looked sideways at him. "Did you really like it?"

"What, your book?"

"Of course, my book! What did you think?"

"Well, I had no idea Aunt Sarah took over after your mother died when you were little. You've never talked about that." He chuckled. "Maybe Aunt Sarah won't like being portrayed as such a tough cookie."

Clara sat up straight. "But I didn't say anything damning, did I?"

"No, not at all. You just wrote a heartfelt story about growing up without your mother. Clara, I don't think you have anything to worry about."

"Then why is everyone so upset?"

"Darned if I know. But it was sure clear last night at dinner that people are worried about something."

Clara nodded. "It's mostly Aunt Sarah, I think."

"What happened to your mother, exactly?" Trey asked. "You were pretty vague about her death."

Clara stared at him. "I was only five. I don't really remember it. My father never talked about it, and neither has Aunt Sarah."

"Hmmm," Trey murmured. He walked into the kitchen just as the phone rang. "Clara," he called. "Miranda wants to know if you can meet her for coffee this morning."

She sighed. After last night's dinner, she wasn't sure she wanted to.

Chapter Eight
Really?

At ten o'clock Clara got dressed and drove downtown to the coffee shop to meet Miranda. She parked in front of Boswell's Bookstore, and as she was walking past it a book cover in the window caught her eye. She stopped to study it. It was a children's book, and what caught her attention was the picture of a little girl sitting on the sidewalk curb. Somehow it was unsettling. She wrenched her attention away and walked into the coffee shop to meet her sister.

Miranda was already sitting at a table with two cups of coffee. "Hi, Clara," she said with a smile.

"Hey, there!" Clara hugged her, then sat down across from her. Miranda always looked so put-together; today she wore jeans and a stylish red tee shirt. She looked younger than Clara felt this morning.

"Dinner last night was a freaking free-for-all," her sister blurted. "I'm sorry the family attacked you."

Clara took a deep breath. "You have no idea how hard publishing this memoir is turning out to be."

Miranda patted her hand. "You'd think it was Aunt Sarah's story you're telling, not your own," she said with a laugh.

Clara sighed. "There is nothing funny about it, Sis. Why is everybody so against me publishing a memoir?"

"I honestly don't know. But it seems to me that Aunt Sarah and Uncle Joe and Uncle Larry all agree about whatever it is."

"My nerves are shot," Clara admitted. "I'm having nightmares about Aunt Sarah, and I'm also having what my doctor says are panic attacks."

Miranda narrowed her eyes. "That's awful, Clara. Why is this so upsetting for you? I'd think publishing a book would be exciting."

Clara hesitated. "You remember how private I always was, don't you? Well, I still am. Now that my memoir is going to be published I am suddenly realizing that I'm exposing myself to the whole world."

Miranda scooted her chair closer. "I'm so sorry, Clarabel. Shame on everyone for making this so painful. If they knew how hard it's turning out to be for you, maybe they would cut it out."

"I'm still going to publish it," Clara said. "It's something I need to do for me."

"Good for you!" Her sister leaned in closer. "Do you want me to read it?"

"Trey read it," Clara admitted.

"And?"

She looked into her sister's eyes and gave her a half-smile. "He said he loved it! He couldn't put it down."

"That's wonderful!"

Clara decided not to tell her that Trey had marked up her pages and how awful it made her feel. She guessed she was feeling over-vulnerable about criticism.

"So," Miranda pursued, "what's next in the publishing process?"

"I have to decide on the cover art."

"You know, Sis, I bet the family will come around eventually."

Clara said nothing, just sipped her coffee. She wished she had Miranda's confidence. "You really think they will?"

After an awkward silence, her sister said softly, "Sure. And I want you to know I'm here to support you."

*   *   *

The next morning Clara put on blue jeans and a long-sleeved blue shirt and nervously drove to her appointment with Dr. Craig. She parked on the street, as instructed, and walked up the steep driveway. By the time she reached the front porch she was short of breath.

A note was taped to the door. "Please let yourself in and sit in the living room."

Clara walked into the house, found a seat on the floral-print sofa, and looked around the room. No family photos. She studied the blue sheet draped over the entrance to what she assumed was another room and resisted the temptation to see what was on the other side. Then she caught sight of something on the beige carpet. Cat hair!

That did it! She got up and peeked behind the blue sheet.

Oh, my God. Not one but three cats were lounging on an overstuffed green chair. She let go of the curtain. Just as Dr. Craig walked into the hallway, Clara sneezed.

"Hello, Clara. Please go on into my office. I'll be right there."

She sneezed again. Should she stay or go? Behind her, Dr. Craig called, "I opened the window so you could get more air."

Clara pulled a Kleenex out of the box on the coffee table and blew her nose.

"I see you parked in the correct spot today," the doctor said.

Clara bit her lip. She wanted to say that she'd seen the three cats in the next room, but she decided against it. Instead she blew her nose again.

"I'm wondering if you are sneezing on purpose," Dr. Craig said. "Maybe avoiding something?"

Clara snapped her mouth shut and pulled out another Kleenex. *I'm sneezing because of your three cats!*

Dr. Craig settled into her chair. "How has this week been for you?"

"I attended a family dinner that was very stressful," Clara began.

"Oh? Tell me about it." She picked up her clipboard.

Clara sneezed again, then gave up. "Dr. Craig, I told you I am allergic to cats, but I see that you have three cats in your house."

The therapist turned widened eyes on her and Clara took a deep breath. "I know you have cats, and you know that I am allergic. I'm afraid I can't continue with our sessions."

Dr. Craig stared at her. "You gave me less than twenty-four hours notice for a cancellation. I will still need to charge you for your time today."

That was too much. "Really? I will pay you for last week's session, but since you misled me about your cats, I am not paying for today."

"Oh. Well, I—"

She searched in her purse and handed the therapist a check she had already made out. Then she marched out the door and down the hallway. Halfway to the front door she stopped and looked back. Dr. Craig was standing in the hall, her arms crossed over her ribcage, her face set.

Clara turned away.

Once back in her Volvo, she dug in her purse for her cell phone and dialed Dr. Stevens, the therapist Mollie had suggested.

A male voice answered. "Dr. Stevens here."

"Oh! I was expecting an answering machine."

He laughed. "I assure you I am a real person. To whom am I speaking?"

"My name is Clara Perkins. My doctor suggested I see someone about my anxiety. And," she added as an afterthought, I am looking for a therapist who does not have a cat!"

He laughed again. "I don't have a cat."

"Not even an outside cat?"

"No, not even an outside cat."

"Well, then, do you have any available appointments?"

"Let me check my calendar," he said calmly. "What about Friday at eleven-thirty?"

He gave her the location of his office. Clara repeated the address, then asked, "This is an office building, right?"

"Why, yes," he said after a slight hesitation.

"Not a private home where cats roam, right?" *Oh, that must sound absurd.* She cleared her throat. "I'm sorry if that sounds like an unusual question, but I'm highly allergic to cats."

"I see."

Her nerves ratcheted up a notch. *He must think I'm nuts!*

* * *

"You're really quiet tonight, Clara," Trey said that night over dinner. "What's on your mind?"

Clara told him about the "cat counselor" and about walking out of her office.

Trey frowned. "She had *three* cats? And she told you she only had one cat and that was an outdoor cat?"

"I'm beginning to think talking about my anxiety with these therapists is a no-win proposition"

Trey nodded. "Are you sure you want to try another one?"

"No, I'm not sure, but I don't know what else to do. I'm not sleeping and I can't eat. I'm really feeling anxious."

"I think it'll all work out, honey. Let's go for a walk and get your mind off everything. I think maybe you'll conquer your anxiety on your own."

They took a long, rambling walk through the neighborhood, but it didn't help much. That night she tossed and turned for hours. Maybe Trey was right. Maybe she would eventually get her anxiety under control on her own.

But around 3 a.m. she woke up with a start. She'd been dreaming that Dr. Craig and Aunt Sarah were shouting at her, telling her to relax, that everything would be okay. And in her dream there were cats. Thousands of cats!

Slowly she climbed out of bed and went into the kitchen for a glass of cold water. *Maybe Trey is right. Maybe I will eventually get control of my anxiety. But maybe, just maybe, Dr. Stevens can speed it up.*

Chapter Nine
Time Will Tell

Friday came. Over breakfast, Clara told Trey about her apprehension about Dr. Stevens. "If this guy doesn't work out ..." Her voice trailed off. She was losing her perspective. Her apprehensive feelings were getting worse, and she was starting to lose weight. Dr. Shu had asked her to keep him posted, but she hesitated to call him.

Later that morning she changed into black slacks and a pink long-sleeved shirt and drove to the other side of town for her appointment. She wore flat shoes in case she had to walk up any steep hills.

Traffic seemed unusually heavy for this hour of the morning in New Millhaven, but she found the two-story office building at the end of Fourth Street and saw that there was plenty of parking in front.

There was no elevator, so Clara walked up a flight of stairs and found the office at the end of a long hallway. In the waiting room a number of chairs were lined up against the wall; she took the first one and sat uneasily until precisely at 11:30 a short, paunchy man appeared wearing brown slacks and a pinstripe shirt.

"Clara Perkins?" he asked in a quiet voice.

Clara rose. "Yes, I'm Clara. Hello, Dr. Stevens."

He pinned her with large brown eyes. "Follow me." In silence he led her to the last room on the long hallway, bent down to turn on the white noise machine, and waved her into his office.

A burgundy sofa sat along the far wall. Less than two feet away was the doctor's black leather chair. Next to the chair a green vine of some sort in a stone pot sprawled onto the floor. It looked so wilted Clara was sure he didn't remember to water it. Another noise machine whirred next to the withered plant.

Across the room she spied a framed diploma on the wall behind the desk, which was piled high with papers. A large paper cup of Starbucks coffee and a bottle of Evian water nestled among the clutter. The window blind, she noted, was completely closed.

She sat down on the edge of the sofa and the doctor settled his short frame into the black leather chair. "I'm Doctor Stevens." He extended his hand and Clara leaned toward him to shake it.

"Clara, why don't you tell me why you've come today?"

"Well," she said slowly, "I am having some issues with anxiety."

He picked up a notepad from the floor beside his chair and jotted something down. "Have you any idea what might be the source of your anxiety?"

For a moment she couldn't think of a thing to say. Then she gave herself a mental shake and swallowed hard. "Well, I think it's associated with a memoir I've written. I'm about to publish it, and I'm feeling very nervous because some members of my family are criticizing me for writing it."

"Is it a negative book about your family?" he asked quickly.

"Oh, no, not in the least. It's nothing like that. It's just about my memories from when I was a little girl and we lost our mother."

He kept writing. "How old were you?"

"Almost five."

"What happened to your mother?" Dr. Stevens asked.

"I really don't know. My family never talked about it. My mother's sister, Aunt Sarah, helped my father raise us."

"Your Aunt Sarah raised you?" He studied his notepad and continued writing.

"Um ... yes. I had older siblings, but it was Aunt Sarah who pretty much raised us. We were, in fact we still are, a very close-knit family. We have dinners as a family once a week, and we keep in touch. Usually my family is supportive of everything I do, but now ..." She swallowed again. "My aunt and her brothers, my uncles, don't want me to publish my memoir. In fact, they're being very negative about it."

"I see."

"And there's something else," she continued. "I've always been a shy person. I've kept to myself and, especially when I was raising my children, I didn't go out much. Even now I go to great lengths to avoid being in the spotlight. So writing this book is a big step for me. Publishing it, putting it out there in the world, feels like coming out of the closet in a way."

"I see," he said again.

"My Aunt Sarah has been really, well, unpleasant about my memoir. She thinks I wrote about things I shouldn't, I guess."

"What things would those be?"

"I don't honestly know." She clasped and unclasped her hands. "I'm not sure my anxiety has anything to do with how critical my aunt is being."

"Has she read your memoir?"

"No, she hasn't. In fact, she refuses to even look at it."

"Ah." Dr. Stevens twiddled his pencil between his fingers. "I had to teach my parents a lesson about life," he said.

Clara stared at him. *What? What a strange thing to say!*

"Parents need boundaries," he added quickly. "Mine still do."

Suddenly she felt uncomfortable. Parents and boundaries? What did that have to do with her anxiety? She started to say something but Dr. Stevens took no notice, just went on talking.

"I am enjoying telling my parents how wrong they were in the way they raised me," he said. "I have to stand up for myself. I am forty-six years old and I just got married for the first time."

That seemed like a really personal bit of information to be telling a therapy patient. Why would he be talking like this about himself?

"I have a wife, now," he said with a smile.

74

Clara edged away from him.

"Parents are the root of all the problems that children have," he continued, raising his voice.

She folded her fingers around her purse strap. "I don't feel that my parents—"

He cut her off. "When I was ten years old I was the smallest kid in my class, and I was bullied. When I fought back at school one day, my parents punished me."

Clara caught her breath. *This guy has real issues with his parents. Is he saying I should blame my parents for my problems?*

"Now," he went on, "my parents can feel what I had to suffer through!"

Clara edged farther away from him. *He's not even listening to me!*

"I will never have any children," he announced. "My wife didn't like that idea at first since she is just twenty-one years old. But she's coming around to my way of thinking."

She blinked. "Your way of thinking?" She must have looked shocked because he suddenly shouted, "What is wrong with marrying a much younger woman?" His voice sounded so accusing she flinched.

Oh, that poor girl, only 21 years old and she's married to this 46-year-old bachelor who's still angry at his parents.

Dr. Stevens leaned forward. "I like to share things about myself in my sessions. You see, I am a real person."

Oh, yes, I see, Clara thought. *I see that you are in desperate need of counseling yourself.*

This man resented his parents when he was young, and now that he is an adult he feels the need to punish them.

She sat in stunned silence while he bragged about his fine education and how successful he was with his therapy practice. "You know, my father is also a therapist," he confided.

Clara nodded. "No, I did not know that." Surreptitiously she glanced down at her watch. He rambled on and on, and she kept inching farther and farther away from him. Finally, *finally*, he looked over at her.

"You have grown very quiet," he said. "We'll have to find out exactly what happened with *your* parents next time. I have lots of appointments open all next week."

Of course he has lots of appointments open! People probably come to see him once and they never come back.

"So, what day next week works for you?"

She couldn't believe he actually thought she would continue with this. "I'll call you," she said quickly. But she knew she would not be returning. What a waste of time! She walked to the door and didn't look back.

The minute she climbed into her car she covered her face with her hands. *Ohmigod, that guy is nuts! Are all therapists crazy? How am I going to explain another wacky doctor to Trey? Or Dr. Shu?*

76

She took a few deep breaths to calm herself down, then decided to stop by The Tea Leaf, have a quiet cup of coffee, and collect her thoughts.

When she walked in, Mollie was sitting at a table reading a magazine. How uncanny! It was Mollie who had recommended Dr. Stevens in the first place!

Mollie glanced up. "Clara! You look upset."

"Do I?" She sank onto the empty chair.

"Yes, you do. Have you seen Dr. Stevens yet?"

Clara bit her lip. "Yes, I have. And you won't believe what happened." She told Mollie everything, including that the middle-aged Dr. Stevens had just married a 21-year-old girl."

"Holy cow," Mollie murmured. "That's really creepy."

"It's more than 'creepy', Mollie. Telling me all that personal stuff is really inappropriate!"

Mollie nodded and sipped her tea. "I found out my brother stopped seeing Dr. Stevens last week."

"I'm not a bit surprised," Clara said. "You should have said something."

"What are you going to do now?"

Clara closed her eyes. "I have absolutely no idea. I've seen three therapists now. All of them were kind of odd, and none of them helped me with my anxiety."

When she left the coffee shop she drove aimlessly around town for an hour, then went home to start dinner. After she had the chicken roasting in the oven along with the baked potatoes, she tossed a green salad together and decided to read her email. There was a note from the cover artist. "What do you think of this?"

She opened the file and stared at the image in horror. A heavily made-up adolescent girl in a tarted-up short skirt and minuscule sequined tee shirt stood under a tree wearing red spike heels.

Oh, my God! No, no, *no*! It was all wrong. She gritted her teeth and began to type furiously. When she finished the message she sat staring at the computer for a long minute, then pressed Send.

At that moment she heard Trey's voice. "Honey, I'm home!"

She collected herself and went to greet her husband.

Later, at dinner, Clara just pushed her food around and around on her plate. Trey watched for a time, then laid his fork down. "Okay, what's up?"

She sucked in a big breath and told him what had happened with Dr. Stevens.

"What?" Trey exploded. "He really said all that stuff about himself and his parents?"

Her eyes welled up. "He certainly did."

"That's terrible. Isn't there someplace to report weird therapists?"

She mopped at her tears with her napkin. "I'm going to call Dr. Shu."

Trey's face tightened. "You know, Clara, you've gone your whole life without this level of anxiety, right up until now. It's all about publishing this book of yours, isn't it?"

"Yes, I guess so."

"It's creating a lot of stress for you, honey. And it's also making your family worry."

"Well, yes it is, but so what? The more I think about that, the madder I get. I'm not going to cave in and do what everybody else wants. It's *my* book, *my* memoir, about *my* life. I wrote it and I'm going to publish it!" She bolted out of her chair and walked into the family room.

Trey followed her. "Clara …"

"Trey, you read my book. You said you liked it. Would you decide not to publish it just because your family objected?"

He thought for a long moment. "No," he said finally. "I would go ahead and publish it."

"All my life it's been hard for me to believe in myself. I've always been afraid somebody won't approve of something I'm doing, or that they will criticize me and hurt my feelings. I think maybe I need to grow thicker skin."

Wow, that's exactly right! I need to grow thicker skin.

Starting right now.

Chapter Ten

Potluck

Clara had just finished typing up the blurb for the back cover of her memoir when the phone on her desk rang. She picked up the receiver to hear her sister Miranda's voice. "Can you pick up Uncle Joe and Aunt Sarah for our potluck in the park? It's this afternoon."

"Sure. I hope Aunt Sarah doesn't go on and on about my book again. Her negativity is really getting to me."

"I'm sure she will, Sis. It's the only thing she talks about these days."

Clara sighed.

"Don't let Aunt Sarah get to you, Clarabel. See you at the park."

It took an hour to re-focus on what she'd been doing, looking at various designs for the front cover of her memoir. Publishing this book was turning out to be more of a hassle than she'd ever dreamed.

On the way to pick up Aunt Sarah, she told Trey about the cover artist's latest ideas. Trey nodded and made sympathetic noises until they arrived at her aunt's house.

Aunt Sarah was waiting on the porch, and when they pulled up she sped down the walk to the car. Thank God she was smiling when she climbed into the passenger seat.

Trey reached over to buckle her seat belt, but she slapped his hand away. "We're picking up Joe, aren't we?" she asked.

"Trey slid into the driver's seat. "Yes, we are."

"Good." After that, Aunt Sarah said nothing.

Clara saw that her aunt was holding a large manila envelope against her chest. She held it tight for the entire five blocks to Uncle Joe's apartment, and when they turned into his driveway, Aunt Sarah surprised them both.

"Let me go fetch him," she announced.

Trey and Clara looked at each other in surprise. Trey opened his door to get out. "Sarah, are you sure? It's really no problem for me to—"

"For heaven's sake, Trey," she snapped. "I'm not a child!" Aunt Sarah grabbed her purse with one hand and scrambled out onto the sidewalk, still pressing the envelope to her chest.

The minute Uncle Joe answered the door she shoved the envelope into his hands. He opened it, glanced at the contents, and then looked up at his sister. Clara thought she saw some papers and what looked like newspaper clippings. He shoved them back in the envelope and disappeared into his apartment, leaving Aunt Sarah waiting at the door. In a few moments he reappeared with a large white manila folder, and the two of them walked toward the car, whispering to each other.

"I wonder what those two are up to," Trey murmured.

Clara took a deep breath. "I hope it's nothing to do with my book. They were both pretty annoyed with me at dinner the other night."

Trey got out to help Aunt Sarah, but she waved him off. "I can get in by myself!"

His eyebrows went up. He glanced at Clara, but she decided not to say anything. She didn't want to set Aunt Sarah off again, so she got out of the car and helped Uncle Joe into the back seat next to her.

"Thank you, child," he said with a smile. "Is Larry coming to the picnic?"

"Yes, I think so."

Uncle Joe leaned toward Aunt Sarah in the front seat. "You need to show Larry those papers," he whispered.

"What papers?" Clara asked.

"Mind your own business, dearie," her aunt snapped.

Clara's cheeks grew hot. Suddenly she felt uneasy about tonight's family potluck in the park.

When Trey parked the car, Uncle Larry was standing on the curb, waving to them, and the family was settled at a large picnic table covered with one of Casey's checked tablecloths. Platters of food sat in the center.

Uncle Joe got out of the car and Aunt Sarah and Uncle Larry drew him apart from the others. Trey and Clara walked over to the picnic table, and Casey stood up. "What are the three musketeers doing over there?" she wondered.

Aunt Sarah, looking annoyed about something, folded up the white envelope and stuffed it in her purse. Then she and the uncles took seats at the picnic table.

Miranda looked up at them. "What are you three up to?"

No one answered.

"Oh, well," she said with a shrug. "Let's eat."

Aunt Sarah looked over at Clara. "Clara, I need you to drive me to the bank tomorrow morning. I have to get into my safe deposit box."

Clara frowned. She had a full morning of her own errands. "Could I pick you up after lunch?"

Her aunt pursed her lips, and Uncle Joe looked away.

What is going on?

"Aunt Sarah, if you're still concerned about my memoir, maybe you'd like to read the manuscript?"

"No! Don't you try to give me that awful book of yours. It's full of lies."

"How do you know that? You haven't read a single word of it."

"No, and I don't want to."

"I've read it," Trey volunteered. "It's pretty engaging."

"I'll read it, Clara!" Casey offered, spooning pork and beans from the pot on the table. She reached across the table and touched Clara's hand. "I'd like to read your manuscript, Clara. I'll let you know if it's okay to publish it."

"What?" Clara shouted. "Wait a minute! I don't need anyone's permission to publish my book!"

Aunt Sarah turned pale and glanced sideways at Uncle Joe. "Can she really do that?" he muttered.

"Stop whispering!" Clara shouted. "If you want to know something, just ask me directly."

Trey reached a hand to her shoulder. "Calm down, honey."

"No, I will not calm down!" She jerked to her feet. "I don't need anybody's approval to publish my own memoir."

Aunt Sarah's face went white as paste.

"Aunt Sarah, are you all right?" Miranda asked.

"Yes," she said shortly, "I am fine. Would it matter to Clara if I weren't?"

"Of course it would matter!" Clara said.

"Then prove it. Stop all this book nonsense."

"It's not 'book nonsense," Clara said as calmly as she could manage. "Writing my memoir is something I've always wanted to do, and now I've done it. I think you should all be proud of me."

No one said a word. Clara sat down and in silence spooned a big helping of potato salad onto her plate.

*   *   *

After a restless night, Clara drove to the coffee shop for some time away from her computer and a cup of much-needed coffee. In the parking lot she saw Mollie sitting in her car, and she stepped up to tap on the window.

"Clara!" Mollie exclaimed. "I didn't expect to see you here."

"I had an awful night last night," Clara confessed. "I decided I needed some time out of the house this morning."

"Have you found another therapist yet?"

"My doctor recommended someone, but I'm really unsure about trying anyone else. I'm trying to work up the courage to call her."

Mollie nodded. "I think you'll start to feel better when you find a professional to talk to."

"Maybe."

"Would it help if I told you I believe we have the power within us to overcome difficult things?"

"No, it wouldn't, Mollie. But thanks for the thought. Until my book is finally published, I guess I'm just going to feel a lot of anxiety."

"Is it your family?"

"Not really, no. They're making it difficult because they're so against it and won't say why, but I think it's mostly my fear about exposing myself. Maybe all memoir writers feel this way."

Mollie smiled. "Maybe. But talking to a therapist might help, don't you think?"

"To be honest, after the last three therapists, I'm not really sure. Lord knows I'm apprehensive about it."

She drew in a long, fortifying breath. "Then again, what have I got to lose?"

Chapter Eleven

More Than She Ever Wanted To Know

Clara checked her watch, grabbed her purse, and said goodbye to Mollie.

"Where are you off to?" Mollie asked, looking up from her latte.

"Aunt Sarah's. She needs me to drive her to the bank. To her safe deposit box, actually."

"How is Aunt Sarah?"

"Grumpy."

Mollie laughed. "What else is new?"

Clara rolled her eyes and headed for the door.

This morning Aunt Sarah was wearing a floral dress and tennis shoes, and she was even more grumpy than she had been on the phone. She sat hunched over a bulky looking box, complaining about the weather (too hot), about the neighbor's dog (too loud), and finally about Clara's driving. "You're going too fast." She even complained about the bank. "They should tear down that awful, ugly old building."

Clara said little. Finally they were ushered into the vault with floor-to-ceiling banks of safe deposit boxes. The teller inserted his key and slid out a large grey metal box.

"Now, Clara," her aunt said loudly, "just hand me those envelopes in the blue box and don't watch." She then lifted the metal lid.

Clara handed over the three manila envelopes, but just as her aunt reached for the last one, something slid out and fluttered to the floor. It was a faded newspaper clipping, the paper slightly yellowed. Clara glimpsed the headline. "A Neighborhood Nightmare."

"Give me that!" her aunt ordered.

She scooped it up and Aunt Sarah snatched it out of her hand, jammed it back into the manila envelope, and tried to stuff it into the already overflowing safe deposit box. Clara could see it wasn't going to fit.

"Let's take everything out and try to consolidate it," she suggested.

"No!"

"Please, Aunt Sarah. You can see your envelope won't fit. We need to reorganize everything."

"Oh, all right. But just the envelopes. Here, hold these while I move things around." She handed Clara a jumble of papers and envelopes, then moved to block her view.

But Clara caught a glimpse of an interesting-looking slim maroon velvet case jammed in one corner of the metal box. When her aunt pushed it aside, it rattled.

"What's in that box, Aunt Sarah? Jewelry?"

"Nothing that concerns you, Clara."

"If it's jewelry, you could take it out and wear it on special occasions."

"Mind your own business, girl. It's not jewelry."

"Oh? Well, what is it, then?"

Her aunt didn't answer, just went on reloading the papers and the three manila envelopes she'd brought with her. She didn't say another word until Clara helped her into the Volvo and they pulled out of the parking lot.

Why was her aunt being so secretive about everything? First there were all those boxes in her basement and now these manila envelopes and the maroon velvet case. Her aunt had been more than grumpy lately, downright hostile at times. Clara's instincts told her she was hiding something, but what? Was her mind going funny in her old age?

"Clara," her aunt said when they reached the house. "I need you to move a box for me."

"Again? I thought I moved everything already."

"Don't talk back," her aunt snapped. "Come inside and don't argue."

Inside, Aunt Sarah pointed to one of the two boxes Clara had lugged up the basement stairs just a week ago. "Move that!" her aunt ordered.

"You want it moved back down to the basement?"

"Don't argue, Clara. Just do it."

It wasn't that it was so heavy; it was just an awkward shape, bulky and hard to carry when she couldn't see where she was going. Oh, well. It was clear her aunt couldn't move it by herself. She grabbed it, jockeyed it into her arms, and started down the steps to the basement.

All went well until she had almost reached the bottom step and she tripped over something. She sprawled backwards onto the stairs and sat down so hard an arrow of pain shot up her tailbone. The bulky box went tumbling on down and burst open.

A long, canvas-wrapped object rolled out.

Apparently Aunt Sarah had not heard her fall, so she picked herself up, crept on down the stairs, and walked over to pick up the object. She reached for it and stopped short. What on earth?

Something poked out one end of the canvas-wrapped bundle. Something long and slim and metallic-looking. *Oh, my God, it's a rifle barrel!* What was Aunt Sarah doing with a rifle hidden away in a box in her basement?

Clara stood frozen in place for a good three minutes, wondering all kinds of things. She assumed the gun was old, but she was afraid to unwrap the canvas and look closer. Had it been

Uncle Larry's? Uncle Joe's? Why had her aunt kept it hidden away?

After another minute she decided to re-wrap the rifle and shove it back in the storage box. Quickly she slapped the canvas back over the exposed barrel and carefully laid the weapon back in the cardboard box. Her hands felt sweaty. Then she shoved the box into the darkest corner of the basement, climbed back up the stairs into the kitchen, and peered at Aunt Sarah's face.

Her aunt's pale blue eyes looked perfectly innocent. "Clara, would you like some tea before you go?"

Tea! She needed a stiff bourbon and soda, not tea! She couldn't wait to tell Trey about the rifle she'd found. And about the maroon velvet case in the safe deposit box that was "not jewelry."

She drove straight home. Before she set the table for dinner, she poured a big glass of wine for Trey and one for herself.

"What's the occasion?" her husband asked.

"It's not exactly an occasion. It's what I found in Aunt Sarah's safe deposit box."

His eyebrows went up. "Tell me."

She told him about Aunt Sarah's safe deposit box, about the manila envelopes and the newspaper clipping and the maroon velvet case that rattled. But for some reason she didn't tell him about the box in Aunt Sarah's basement and the rifle barrel she'd accidentally uncovered. She didn't know why, she just didn't want to deal with it right now.

"Well," Trey said in a matter-of-fact tone, "so Aunt Sarah has weird stuff in her safe deposit box. Lots of people keep all kinds of things squirreled away."

Clara took a sip of wine and carefully set her glass on the table. "Okay, but how do you explain all those boxes in her basement that she doesn't want me to look in?"

"Clara, that's the crux of the problem. Your Aunt Sarah wants to keep everything a big secret."

"But what *is* it she wants to keep secret?"

"It's probably nothing much at all," Trey said. "Try not to worry about it."

Well, *that* certainly didn't make her feel better! But maybe she should just accept that she was never going to figure out what was going on with Aunt Sarah. Besides, right now she had her memoir on her mind. Publication, which she thought of as her "coming out party," was just around the corner, and she was feeling more anxious than ever.

* * *

At two o'clock in the morning Clara rolled over in bed and sat up. Moonlight spilled through the bedroom curtains. She'd always done her best thinking at night so she pushed aside the lace panel and looked outside at the garden. Her manuscript was now being formatted, and in just a few weeks it would be printed.

A combination of dread and joy swept over her, and her heart started to race. *This is it*, she thought. This was something she had created herself, out of her own life. She was proud of what she'd done, but she knew the instant her book was published, people would read all about her life and her thoughts and her feelings—everything. She would be exposed.

Then she had to laugh. At least publishing her memoir would keep her mind off Aunt Sarah's strange behavior.

And off that rifle hidden in her basement.

Chapter Twelve

Another Try

Clara drove down Fig Street to check out Dr. Rothman's office, which was next to Futures Bank where Aunt Sarah had her safe deposit box. There it was, a huge brown office complex. She pulled into the parking lot and sat staring at the two-story building.

It was a quiet area. Tall pine trees surrounded the structure, and pink and magenta dahlias bloomed along the fence surrounding the L-shaped structure. Planter boxes with red geraniums were attached to each upstairs window.

The longer she sat in the car the more nervous she got. She watched the people exiting the building and walking toward the parking lot, wondering if one of them was Dr. Teresa Rothman. She had not made an appointment yet because she wanted to check out her office first; after consulting three really strange therapists she was feeling very cautious. Besides, she wanted to check for cats.

She got out of the Volvo and walked inside, past the receptionist's desk. A few steps beyond the first office on the right she spied a door with a metal nameplate. Teresa Rothman, Ph.D.

Through the window blinds she saw a woman sitting behind a large desk.

She scanned the room for a cat. At that moment the receptionist behind the desk raised her head and Clara quickly stepped out of sight. She retraced her steps down the stairs and into the parking lot. Not one cat, she thought with relief.

Back in her car she dug her cell phone out of her purse, took a deep breath, and dialed Dr. Rothman's number. She waited until the end of the recorded message, and at the beep, she started talking.

"This is Clara Perkins. I would like to schedule an appointment with Dr. Rothman." She gave her cell phone number and hung up. There, she'd done it! She started the Volvo and was just backing out of her space when a red Volkswagen with the sunroof open came flying toward her.

She slammed on the brakes and stared at the driver, a woman with her hair in a ponytail arranged high on one side of her head and tied with a pink bow. The woman got out of her car, her cell phone glued to her ear, and bent down to pick up a handful of papers she'd dropped. She was heavy-set and wore a pink and grey jogging outfit.

The woman trotted past her and disappeared into the building. Clara was inching her Volvo out of the parking space when her cell phone buzzed.

"This is Dr. Rothman, returning your call."

"Oh. Um … I'd like to make an appointment. My doctor suggested I talk to someone about my anxiety attacks."

"How about this Friday at one-thirty?"

"Tomorrow?" Clara said in surprise.

"Yes, tomorrow. Does that work for you?"

"Well, yes." She hesitated. "I— I have to ask you something first."

"Yes, what is it?" Dr. Rothman sounded puzzled.

She gripped the steering wheel. "I know this might sound ridiculous, but you don't have a cat in your office, do you?"

"No, I have no cats in my office," Dr. Rothman assured her.

"No cats inside and no cats outside that might come inside?"

The doctor laughed. "No. Let me guess, you have an issue with cats?"

"I'm highly allergic," Clara said firmly.

"Oh, I see. No, there are no cats or dogs here at my office. Only people."

Clara sighed with relief. "All right, I will be there tomorrow." She hung up and pulled out onto the street. Good, no cats. Maybe Dr. Rothman was going to work out.

*   *   *

That evening at dinner Trey put his knife and fork down and reached across the table to take Clara's hand. "What's the matter, honey? You haven't touched anything on your plate."

Clara looked up. Should she tell him she'd arranged to see another therapist? "I guess my mind is on my book," she said finally. That wasn't the whole truth, but it was close enough.

"Oh, yeah?" Trey said over a mouthful of mashed potatoes.

"I'm getting nervous about what to expect when it's finally published."

"It's been sent to the printer, right?"

She gulped down a swallow of water. "Yes. It will be available in just a few weeks. Then bookstores can order copies."

"Bookstores!"

"Well of course, bookstores. How else are people going to buy copies?"

"Are you going to have a book signing?"

She gulped another swallow of water. "I don't know. I think you have to be invited to hold an event like that. But I've already ordered postcards to send to my friends and to the family."

Trey's eyebrows shot up. "You're going to send cards to your family? Even knowing how they feel?"

Clara sighed. "Yes, I am. This is a big accomplishment for me, and I want to share it."

"Aren't you worried about how your family might react? Especially Aunt Sarah?"

Yes, she was extremely apprehensive about her family's reaction; she was especially concerned about Aunt Sarah. But she wasn't going to let it keep her from publishing her memoir. She wouldn't let her aunt's disapproval keep her from standing up for herself. Thank God she'd called Dr. Rothman this afternoon. She needed all the support she could get.

Clara had just started washing the dishes when Mollie telephoned.

"Clara, is everything okay? You missed our coffee date this afternoon."

"What? Oh, gosh, Mollie, I forgot all about it. I was checking out Dr. Rothman's office, and then I worked up my courage and made an appointment with her."

"Oh, you did." Mollie's voice sounded oddly flat. "Well, I sure hope she's a good choice."

"What? You were the one who told me to try again." There was a long silence. "Mollie?"

"Oh, Clara, I think I've made a terrible mistake.

A have a friend who just told me she didn't like Dr. Rothman at all. In fact—"

"Mollie, for heaven's sake, you should have said something."

"I'm sure Dr. Rothman is just fine, Clara. Very professional and … well, very professional."

Clara felt cold all over. "No, you're not sure, Mollie. You're not sure about Dr. Rothman at all, are you?"

"Okay, I'm not."

Clara gritted her teeth. "Mollie, you're a good friend, but you've done me a real disservice."

"Oh, I'm really sorry. I had no idea you were going to make an appointment so soon."

Her heart started to race and she could feel her face flushing. "I need to go, Mollie. I'll call you soon."

* * *

That night Clara tossed and turned, unable to relax. At three o'clock in the morning she woke up, gasping for breath, and grabbed Trey's arm.

"Clara? Clara, are you okay?"

She shook her head. "I just had the weirdest dream, Trey. I dreamed I saw my book in the bookstore. People were laughing at me, and Aunt Sarah was pointing her finger at me and screaming, 'I told you so! I told you so!' I woke up because my heart was pounding so hard."

"Try to relax, Clara. It was just a dream."

She took deep breaths until her heart calmed down. Trey patted her shoulder, rolled over, and began to snore. How does he do that? she wondered. She felt so alone when he just rolled away from her like that.

She was sweating and so short of breath she couldn't get back to sleep. She lay awake until the sky outside the bedroom window turned pink, and then she sat up. She needed to talk to someone.

And then she groaned. Oh, no. Dr. Rothman.

On the way to the doctor's office she stopped at Boswell's Bookstore to talk to the manager. She walked past the tables of newly released books and stopped at the cash register. "May I speak to the manager?"

The girl scanned the store. "Anyone know where Barb is?" she yelled.

Heads turned, and then a woman in her sixties walked forward. She had brown hair with purple highlights around her face with a few pink strands mixed in; she wore jeans and a tee shirt that read Save the Bees, Plant Flowers.

"What can I do for you?"

"I was here a few weeks ago when the author of *Murder in New Millhaven* had a book signing. I was wondering if I could do a book signing here, too."

"Do you live here in New Millhaven?"

"Yes. For over twenty years."

The manager studied her. "Could I see your book cover?"

Clara got out her laptop. "My book is a memoir. It's being printed now, but I have a copy of the cover art right here."

Barb smiled. "Do you plan to advertise this book signing?"

"Yes, I do. I've ordered promotional postcards to mail out to people."

"And can you put an announcement in the newspaper, too? Just send a press release to the book editor."

Suddenly Clara began to get excited. "It sounds like there's a lot that goes into holding a book signing."

The manager laughed. "Holding the book signing is easy. It's selling your book that's hard."

In the next instant Clara started to feel nervous and began to perspire. "Oh."

"Let's plan on Saturday afternoon five weeks from now," Barb said. "That's right in the middle of our busiest season."

When Clara left the store her heart was pounding. Did I really just arrange for a book signing? Just like a real author? Right away she started to worry. Everything would go wrong. Her postcards wouldn't arrive in time. The books wouldn't be printed on schedule. She swallowed. A thousand things could happen.

Thank God she was seeing Dr. Rothman in an hour. She could feel an anxiety attack coming on right this minute!

Chapter Thirteen
You Did What?

Feeling more than a little apprehensive, Clara drove down the winding roadway to Fig Street, turned into the huge brown office complex, and put the Volvo in park. A long look in the rear view mirror told her there was no hiding the bags under her eyes from her sleepless night. She sighed and climbed out of the car.

The receptionist looked at her over the counter. "May I help you?"

"I'm Clara Perkins. I have an appointment to see Dr. Rothman."

The girl gathered up a clipboard, a pen, and a stack of papers. "Just fill these out, please."

Clara thumbed through the stack of pages. "Are you kidding?" she murmured to herself. "I'll be here for an hour filling all this out."

The receptionist overheard her. "Don't worry if it's not all completed before your appointment," she chirped. Clara nodded, chose a chair in one corner, and started on the paperwork. Twenty minutes passed and she was only halfway through the questionnaire.

Down the hallway a door opened and a young woman stepped out of an office, crying. An older woman, with a pony tail on the side of her head, followed her. Oh, God, it was the same woman Clara had seen yesterday in the parking lot! Today her pony tail was tied with a purple bow and she wore a lavender tennis skirt and purple tennis shoes.

The doctor followed the weeping woman to the receptionist's counter and instructed her to make another appointment for the following day.

"Excuse me, doctor" the receptionist said, "remember that tomorrow is Saturday."

"I know, I know. Put her down for one o'clock." She disappeared back down the hallway and shut her office door.

After another 20 minutes, Clara looked up to see the pony-tailed woman standing before her. "You must be Clara." She extended her hand. "I'm Dr. Rothman. Please come back to my office."

Taking her paperwork with her, Clara walked past a room with a refrigerator, a sink, and a small table with two chairs. Must be a lunch room, she thought. At the far end of the hall, she entered the doctor's office. The huge window was open, and Clara could hear the sound of water. Sure enough, when she peeked out, a path lined with rocks and flowers circled alongside the building and a waterfall was splashing into a shallow pool.

Inside, a large leather sofa sat next to a bookcase, and an overgrown ivy plant trailed from a planter on top of the bookcase along the wall. Floor-to-ceiling cupboards flanked an oversized oak desk, each cupboard door marked with a letter of the alphabet. Soda cans, bottled water, and fruit drink bottles cluttered the desktop, along with a large bowl of Hershey's kisses.

Dr. Rothman smiled. "Please take a seat wherever you feel comfortable." Clara chose the brown sofa across from the doctor, who sat rocking back and forth in a black leather chair. Her purple tennis shoes barely reached the floor, and Clara noticed that the shoelaces were pink.

"So, Clara, what brings you to see me today?"

Clara scooted forward, placed her purse on the floor, and folded her hands in her lap. "Well, lately I've been having a lot of anxiety."

Dr. Rothman studied her. "Anxiety about what?" She leaned forward to retrieve the clipboard and pen on her desk.

Clara's heart began to race and she twisted her wedding band around and around on her finger. "I think it has something to do with a book I've written."

"Oh? What kind of book is it?"

"It's a memoir, about when I was a child."

"Why do you think you're feeling anxious about that?"

"Well, up until now my family has always been very supportive of things I've done. Now all of a sudden they're not happy that I've written this book."

"Are you looking for their approval?" the doctor asked.

"Not exactly, no. But they're being very critical and it's affecting my confidence."

"Why do you think that is, Clara?"

Clara swallowed. "All my life I've stayed home and raised my children. I supported my husband in his profession, but I always stayed in the background. Now all of a sudden I'm going to be out in the public eye. I think I'm nervous about it."

"Your entire family is objecting? Including your husband?"

"No. Mostly it's my Aunt Sarah."

"Why do you think she objects, Clara?"

She thought for a moment. "I really have no idea. Maybe Aunt Sarah thinks I wrote something critical about her or revealed some family secret."

Dr. Rothman jotted something down on the clipboard. "Has your aunt read your memoir?"

"No, that's just it," Clara explained. "Aunt Sarah actually refuses to read it!"

The doctor frowned. "Do you have a copy of your book?"

"Yes, I have a working manuscript in my car."

"All right. This is what I want you to do, Clara. I want you to bring me the manuscript so I can read it. That way I can talk with you about it objectively. And I want you to come back next Monday."

"Do you think you can help me with the anxiety I'm feeling? I've had two panic attacks, at least that's what my doctor calls them."

"Yes," Dr. Rothman said decisively, "I can help you."

Clara sighed with relief. "I'll go get my manuscript." When she returned, Dr. Rothman accepted the pages with a smile, and Clara made an appointment for Monday afternoon.

When she got back in the Volvo, her heart was beating so fast she felt dizzy. *Oh, I hope I'm doing the right thing, letting her read my book.*

She sat in her car for a long time, breathing deeply. *What if Dr. Rothman agrees with Aunt Sarah that I shouldn't publish my memoir?*

That night Clara dreamed she was flying in an airplane somewhere and the stewardess was passing out her memoir for all the passengers to read. From the lavatory she overheard people talking about it, and when she walked back to her seat, everyone was laughing at her. Trey was in the dream, and even *he* was laughing!

She woke up short of breath and sweating, so she made herself get out of bed and go to the kitchen for a glass of cold water. She stood at the sink sipping it and tried to calm down.

Did all authors go through this nerve-racking self-doubt?

Chapter Fourteen
Just Getting Started

The closer Clara got to her appointment with Dr. Rothman the more jumpy her nerves grew. What if Dr. Rothman thinks I should stop publication? What if ... what if ...?

She was beginning to wonder whether she was going to live through this.

When she climbed into the Volvo on Monday all at once she felt hot and sweaty so she turned the air conditioning up full blast. It blew her hair all over her face, and when she parked the car she reached into her purse for a hairbrush.

Oh, no! All she could find was an old toothbrush! Well, it *was* funny, but it sure didn't *feel* funny. She peered in the rear view mirror and used the toothbrush to carefully comb her hair.

Inside Dr. Rothman's waiting room she dug out her checkbook, wrote a check for $90 to cover her last session, and handed it to the receptionist.

"Sorry," the girl said. "Dr. Rothman's rates have gone up. They are now one-hundred fifty dollars per session."

"But—" Clara frowned. "Dr. Rothman told me last Friday the charge would be ninety dollars an hour."

The receptionist handed her check back. "I'll have to discuss that with Dr. Rothman."

How dare she raise her rates without telling me! She sat down in the waiting room and tore the check into tiny pieces.

The door at the end of the hallway opened and Dr. Rothman followed a tall, middle-aged man out to the reception area.

Clara watched as the receptionist followed the doctor back to her office, and then she heard them whispering. She guessed it was about the change in rates.

"Let me take care of it," Dr. Rothman said. The receptionist then walked back to her desk and after a moment Dr. Rothman appeared and motioned Clara into her office. Today the doctor wore a black jogging suit with a wide pink stripe down each leg and white tennis shoes with pink shoelaces. Her rather odd hairdo was pulled to one side of her head with a pink bow. *This woman has a thing for pink!*

"How are you today, Clara?"

"Um, excuse me, Dr. Rothman, but there is a discrepancy in your fees that we need to talk about."

"Oh, that. Ignore it. I am only charging you ninety dollars per visit. But of course if the session runs over, there will be overtime fees."

"Overtime? I understood that my session would be just an hour."

"Well, let's say we go fifteen minutes over. In that case I would charge you for an extra half hour. Don't worry, I keep track of the time."

"But you don't start charging until I sit down in your office, right?"

"Oh, no. I actually start charging when you enter the waiting room."

On edge, Clara nervously clasped her hands in her lap.

"So," the doctor continued, "where were we? How are you today, Clara?" She smoothed the yellow notepad in her hand.

Clara's heart began to race. "I'm fine," she lied.

Dr. Rothman rocked back in her black chair until her toes lifted off the floor. "Clara, I have to tell you that I read your book in one sitting. I couldn't put it down! My, you certainly *are* a writer."

Her heart thumped hard. "Do you really think so?"

The doctor nodded. "I have never counseled a real writer before," she said. "Well, aside from myself, of course. I did write my Ph.D. thesis."

"Oh," Clara said.

"People tell me all the time that they are writers," Dr. Rothman added. "Then I read their work and it's so awful I can't get through it."

"Oh," Clara said again.

"I was really interested in the description of your family and the loss of your mother at such a young age. And all those siblings!"

Clara moved to the edge of her seat.

"What happened to your Aunt Sarah?" the doctor pursued. "Is she still alive? What about your uncles? Are you close to your sisters? Are you writing a sequel?"

Clara sighed. So many questions! "Yes, Aunt Sarah is still alive. My aunt is the reason I came to see you in the first place, if you remember."

The doctor's face reddened. "Oh, yes. Yes, of course I remember."

Clara wondered if she really did remember. "If you recall, I am having anxiety attacks."

Dr. Rothman nodded and sent her an exasperated look. "Well, then, let's talk about that."

Clara swallowed. "Did … did you find anything in my memoir that would be upsetting to my family? Especially my aunt?"

"No. Nothing that I could see. Your Aunt Sarah does come off as a very strong-willed woman. Do you think your characterization of your aunt would upset her?"

She drew in a deep breath. "I don't know. As I told you, Aunt Sarah won't tell me what is bothering her about my memoir, and she refuses to read it."

"From what I read you were close to your sister Miranda. Are you still close to her?"

"Yes."

"Maybe Miranda could ask your aunt what her objection is," Dr. Rothman suggested.

"I have already asked her. Miranda has no idea, either."

"Has Miranda read the book?"

Clara shook her head. "No, she hasn't."

"Why not?"

She bit her lip. "When Aunt Sarah and the family made such a fuss about it, telling me I couldn't write about the family and then refusing to even read the book, I decided that none of them was going to read it until it was in print."

"Why is that?"

"It's *my* story, about *my* life. I don't want anyone telling me to change it."

The doctor nodded, picked up a pen, and scratched something across the yellow pad. "So, tell me, was Aunt Sarah living with your family when your mother was still alive?"

Clara frowned. "All I remember is that when I was little Aunt Sarah was always around, especially after Mama died."

"How old were you when your mother died?"

"I had just turned five."

Dr. Rothman asked more questions about the family, how old they were, where they lived, and how they got along with each other. Clara explained everything in detail, but when she looked up, the doctor's eyes were closed. She was sound asleep!

She cleared her throat loudly. Dr. Rothman jerked awake and went on writing on the notepad as if nothing had happened.

Finally Clara glanced at the clock on the desk. "Oh, Dr. Rothman, you didn't tell me my hour was up!"

The doctor looked embarrassed. "I guess I got so involved in listening to your story I lost track of the time. I'll only charge you … let's say one-hundred fifty dollars for today."

"Wait a minute," Clara protested. "You can't charge me a different amount every time I come in!"

"Oh, well, you're right, of course. Next time we'll keep it to just the one hour, I promise."

Clara stood up and moved toward the door, but the doctor stopped her. "I think you should come in again this week," she said.

"Won't next week be soon enough?"

"No. Come in on … Friday."

"Do you really think that's necessary?"

Dr. Rothman blinked. "Yes, I do. Most definitely. We're just getting started."

*   *   *

Clara stopped at the grocery store where she ran into Mollie in the vegetable aisle.

"Oh, Clara, hello."

"I just came from Dr. Rothman's office," Clara said.

Mollie glanced sideways at her. "Me, too. I just came from an hour with my therapist."

The two of them locked gazes. "I'll tell if you will," Mollie teased. "I don't think my therapist is doing me much good."

"I haven't been with mine long enough to tell," Clara said. "But some things are really puzzling."

Mollie nodded, then suddenly grinned. "Let's stop and think a minute, Clara. We're mature women. We know the ways of the world. Maybe we don't need to talk with therapists about the difficulties in our lives."

"Maybe we don't," Clara said somberly. "But I'm not sure my anxiety attacks are over."

When she got back to the house, a big cardboard box was sitting on her front porch. She dragged it into the hallway and cut it open. "My postcards!"

Trey stepped in and looked over her shoulder. She handed him a card and waited expectantly.

"Oh, wow, honey. I really like your book cover!"

"Read the back," she said excitedly.

Trey turned the card over and read aloud. "After her mother's death, Clara grows up right before your eyes. Through her stories you learn what it's like to be the youngest member of a very large family. Clara cherishes her memories of being a little girl, and the reader will experience her life as she did, as a wonderful adventure. You will cheer for her."

Trey hugged her. "This is great! I like the cover picture of the little girl in the red tennis shoes. I guess that's supposed to be your mother, standing behind you in the apron?"

"Yes," she said with a smile. "I finally got the cover artist to understand what I wanted."

"Clara, I'm really proud of you!"

All at once she felt like crying. She'd done it! She had accomplished something she'd wanted to do for years and years. She blinked hard and gave Trey a kiss.

After dinner, Trey retreated to the family room to watch TV and read the newspaper, and Clara telephoned Mollie.

"My postcards have arrived, and they're beautiful!"

"Oh, Clara, congratulations! If you meet me at the coffee shop tomorrow I'll help you address them."

"Great. Ten o'clock?"

"Sure. See you at The Tea Leaf."

The next morning Clara collected all the mailing addresses she'd collected and the postage stamps she'd bought and put them in a folder, then took it and the box with 300 cards and loaded them in the back seat of her car. When she walked back into the house for her car keys, her phone was ringing.

"Hi, Clara, it's Barb from the bookstore. I have good news and bad news."

Her heart dropped right down to her toes. "What's the bad news?"

"We need to change the date of your book signing. Would a week earlier be okay?"

Clara glanced at the calendar by the telephone. "Sure."

"Great! Now here's the good news. At your book signing we'd like you to talk to the audience for a few minutes before you actually start signing copies."

Clara almost choked. "You want me to talk? In front of people?"

Barb laughed. "Yes, in front of people. Then you can just sit and relax behind the table and sign your books."

Suddenly she was short of breath. "Um … talk about what?"

"Oh, you know. How you started writing, what your book is about, that sort of thing."

Now her heart was really starting to pound. The thought of getting up in front of a group of people made her sick with fear. The only public speaking she'd ever done in her life was announcing to her daughter's third-grade class that she had brought two kinds of cupcakes, lemon and chocolate.

"Clara? Are you still there?"

"Yes, Barb, I'm still here." Her voice shook.

"Well, would you give a short talk?"

Clara waited a long, long time before answering. "Y-yes. I think I could do that."

That night she woke up in a panic, her heart racing. She'd been dreaming, but all she could remember about it was standing in front of hundreds of people, feeling sick to her stomach and unable to speak a word. People started whispering and pointing at her, and then Aunt Sarah was there, screaming something, and Uncle Larry was pointing a rifle at her.

She sat straight up in bed. A rifle! Like the rifle in Aunt Sarah's basement! *Why am I thinking about that gun now?*

Sweat soaked her nightgown and she couldn't stop trembling. She should have told Trey about the gun when she'd found it in Aunt Sarah's basement, but she hadn't wanted to even think about it, much less talk about it.

Her dream was all mixed up, but she knew something about that gun was important.

But what was it?

Chapter Fifteen

Butterflies

Clara had been up for hours before Trey walked into the kitchen. He poured himself a cup of coffee and came over to stand by her chair. "You sure tossed and turned last night. What's wrong?"

She settled in a chair, tucked her feet under her, and took a deep breath. "Remember the last time I went over to Aunt Sarah's to move some boxes for her?"

Trey took a sip of coffee. "Yeah, I remember. What about it?"

"Well, when I was carrying a heavy box down to the basement I tripped and fell on the stairs. The box split open."

"So?"

"Trey, there was a rifle in that box!"

He choked on a swallow of coffee. "A what?"

"A rifle. I found a rifle in that box in Aunt Sarah's basement. It was wrapped in canvas, and when the box came open, the barrel was pointed right at me."

Holding onto his coffee cup with one hand, Trey hugged her with his free arm. "Calm down, honey. It's Aunt Sarah's problem, not yours."

"Thank God it wasn't loaded!" she muttered.

Trey put his cup down on the kitchen counter. "How do you know it wasn't?"

She gasped. "I just assumed it wasn't loaded. I covered it back up with the canvas and moved the box into the farthest corner of the basement."

Trey nodded. "Why are you so upset about finding this rifle? Seems to me if it's safe in Aunt Sarah's basement it's none of our business. Lots of elderly people have family guns. They pass them down for generations."

"It just gives me the shivers. I was really freaked out when I found it."

"Hey, take it easy, Clara. You know how secretive Aunt Sarah is. Apparently she doesn't want any of us to know about it. I think you should forget about it."

"I can't. Something about it just doesn't seem right."

"Yeah, maybe you're right about that. But look, Clara, it's really Aunt Sarah's business, not ours. She doesn't know you found it, so I'd try to forget about it."

But she couldn't forget about it. She still felt shaken by last night's dream, and all morning she couldn't stop thinking about that rifle. Did Uncle Larry know about it? Or Uncle Joe? Should she ask them about it and risk more of her aunt's anger?

Trey left for work and Clara stacked the coffee mugs in the dishwasher. She wished she knew what to do. Sometimes she felt really alone.

*   *   *

At ten o'clock Clara drove to The Tea Leaf to meet Mollie. The parking lot was jam-packed, and the only parking space she found was next to Boswell's Bookstore. She dug the box of postcards out of the back seat and started for the coffee shop, but when she passed Boswell's and saw the window display, she stopped dead in her tracks. Taped to the glass was a big photograph of herself and a picture of her book cover. Next to that was a big poster.

MEET CLARA PERKINS, AUTHOR OF
LITTLE GIRL IN RED SHOES ON DECEMBER 8
FROM 2 TO 4 P.M. CLARA WILL TALK ABOUT HER
MEMOIR BEFORE THE BOOK SIGNING.

Her face felt hot and she knew she was flushing. Oh, Lord, was this really happening?

Through the window she saw Barb, giving her a thumbs-up. Clara smiled and waved hello, then stuck her head inside the door. "Barb, where did you get the photo of me? And my book cover?"

"Your photo came from the Internet," Barb said with a grin. "And I got your book cover when you showed it to me and I made a copy, remember?"

"I guess so. It all seems kind of unreal. Thanks, Barb." She tried to sound appreciative, but inside, a battalion of butterflies were zooming around in her stomach.

"When will you get copies of your book?" Barb asked.

"Next week, I hope."

"Bring me twenty to start with. I'll put them on display at the front of the store, along with the other new releases." She pointed to the table by the door.

Clara gulped and managed to nod. "At the front of the store," she murmured. You couldn't walk into the bookstore and miss seeing her memoir. Oh, God, she hoped Aunt Sarah wouldn't visit the bookstore anytime soon.

She walked on to the coffee shop, her heart banging away inside her chest.

Dressed in jeans and a yellow tee shirt, Mollie sat nursing a cup of coffee when Clara plopped her postcards down on the table and slid into the chair across from her.

"What's up, Clara? You're all flushed."

"I'm giving a talk at my book signing in a few weeks at Boswell's Bookstore. There's an announcement in the window already."

"That's great!" Mollie exclaimed.

Clara sucked in a breath. "It doesn't feel so great. Gosh, Mollie, what if no one shows up?"

"I'll come, Clara. Trey will come, and your family will come to support you."

"Oh, my God, my family. And Aunt Sarah!" She closed her eyes.

"Clara, your face is getting really red. Are you okay?"

She clapped her hands on her cheeks. "It's just nerves."

Mollie picked up one of her postcards. "I love your book cover. Very sweet. I especially like the little girl sitting on the curb wearing those red tennis shoes."

Mollie turned the card over and read the back. "Wow, I can't wait to read this!"

Clara surreptitiously wiped the perspiration from her forehead with the back of her hand. For the next two hours they addressed postcards, and then Mollie had to leave, so Clara addressed the rest of her postcards by herself.

It took all afternoon, and when she finally got home, Trey took one look at her and gave her a hug. "You look exhausted. Have you been at Aunt Sarah's?"

She sat down next to him on the sofa and tucked her feet underneath her. "Not today. I was busy addressing postcards with Mollie."

"Is that why you look so stressed?"

"I do?"

"You do. You were frowning when you walked in."

"They moved my book signing up a week. It's next Saturday."

"Good. I know you're nervous about it. It'll be good to get it over with."

"And Barb, at the bookstore, wants me to give a talk before the book signing. You know how I hate getting up in front of people."

"You'll do fine, honey. Don't worry about it."

Clara clenched her teeth. That didn't help much. Trey was used to speaking in public because of his work, but she had been a stay-at-home mom for over 30 years.

What was I thinking when I decided to write a memoir? Even worse, having it published!

"Trey, let's go out for dinner tonight. Some place where I can order a great big drink with swizzle sticks and pink parasols and a lot of rum."

He laughed, but she felt like screaming!

Chapter Sixteen
Out of Line?

On her way to Dr. Rothman's office, Clara stopped at the post office to mail her postcards. Dropping them off gave her a sense of accomplishment, but it also sent a nagging feeling of doubt into her stomach. Her book would be published in just one week! And then there would be the book signing. And ... She gulped down a flash of panic ... her talk.

She sat in the doctor's waiting room for an extra-long time, and after 20 minutes she checked her watch. Apparently Dr. Rothman was running behind. Or maybe the current client's session was running over. She wondered if this happened often.

After another half hour passed, she started to get really nervous. Had she gotten the day wrong? The time of her appointment? Then the doctor's office door opened and an older woman with a young child walked out. When they left the waiting room, Dr. Rothman appeared. Today she wore an orange jumpsuit with a hood and yellow tennis shoes with pink shoelaces.

"Come in, Clara."

Clara took a seat on the sofa near the open window and waited while Dr. Rothman seated herself in the black leather chair.

"Well, Clara, what's new?"

"I'm feeling really uneasy. I mailed the postcard announcements of my book signing this morning."

"Oh?" The doctor looked up from her yellow notepad. "When is your book signing?"

"Next Saturday, at Boswell's Bookstore. I'm getting really nervous."

"How many people do you expect?"

"I sent out two hundred cards to people I know. If only half of them show up, that's an audience of over a hundred."

"Wow, that's a lot of people!"

Clara gave a little groan. "And I just found out that the bookstore manager wants me to give a talk before the book signing."

"Wonderful, Clara!"

"It doesn't feel wonderful, Dr. Rothman. It feels really, really scary."

"Oh, Clara, there's nothing to it. First you make out cue cards with what you want to say. Keep it short and sweet. Then you show your book and tell the audience where they can find it. Then you give a short description of it."

Clara wondered how the doctor knew all this if she had never published a book. She was about to ask when Dr. Rothman dug the box with her manuscript pages out of a desk drawer.

"Here's your manuscript. I forgot to give it back to you at our last session."

Clara glanced inside the box and gasped. The first page was all marked up in red pen, lines crossed out and different words substituted, paragraphs moved around. There were even notes written in the margins! She glanced at the next page, and the next … same thing. Red pen marks everywhere.

How dare she do this?

"You can thank me later," the doctor said.

"I beg your pardon? Why did you do this? I didn't give you permission to mark up my manuscript. My book was already edited!"

Dr. Rothman bent over her notepad and did not look up. "I thought it needed another pair of eyes."

"You should have asked me first," Clara said firmly.

"Oh, yes, of course. I just thought …" Dr. Rothman's face turned slightly pink. "Um … now don't you worry, Clara. I will help you every step of the way."

"Excuse me? I came here so you could help me with my anxiety, not edit my book!"

An awkward silence fell. Finally the doctor shrugged and glanced up at her. "Are you having a dinner get-together after your book signing?"

"I hadn't thought that far ahead."

"I'll help you put it together at a restaurant close to Boswell's. We can keep it to just family, and that way I can meet them all."

Dr. Rothman rattled on, but Clara was starting to feel really uneasy. "Talk it over with your husband," the doctor said. "See what he thinks about it. But the sooner you make reservations …" Her voice trailed off.

"Wait just a minute, Dr. Rothman."

But the doctor had picked up her cell phone and was typing something on the mini-keyboard. "I'm looking for a restaurant next to Boswell's for you."

Clara stood up. "I can take care of that myself," she said in a clipped tone.

The doctor put the phone down and reached for the coffee cup on her cluttered desk. "I'm afraid our time is up, Clara. Let's talk again on Wednesday."

"Dr. Rothman, I don't think—"

"If we're going to get to the bottom of your anxiety, we will need to talk a lot before your book signing. I'll see you Wednesday at two o'clock."

Clara turned and walked out. Back in her car she thumbed through the rest of her manuscript. Every single page had lines taken out, wording changed, notes written all over it. On the last page was a pink post-it note: "Dear Clara, I am so excited to be working with you on your book! I am available to talk about it any time at no extra charge. Here is my cell phone number. Teresa Rothman."

She stared at the note for a long minute. Since when does a therapist get involved with editing a client's book? Was Dr. Rothman just trying to be helpful, or was she really out of line?

She drove home and threw the marked-up manuscript pages in the trash can. Then she spent an hour arranging for a small dinner at Restaurante Italiano. Just as she hung up the phone, Trey appeared in the kitchen.

"Honey, you look awfully serious. What's up?"

"I'm arranging for a dinner gathering after my book signing next week, but I just had an upsetting session with Dr. Rothman and now I'm getting nervous."

Trey nodded sympathetically, and then the phone rang. "Aunt Sarah!"

Trey handed her the receiver and Clara's heart somersaulted into her stomach.

"So," her aunt said, "I see you're having a book signing."

"Yes, I am. I hope you will come."

There was a long silence, and then her aunt spoke in a tight voice. "Just remember this, Clara. You can't take back something once it's revealed."

"Aunt Sarah, what do you mean? Tell me!"

The line went dead.

A sick feeling bloomed in the pit of Clara's stomach. "Trey, Aunt Sarah said something about not being able to take back something once it's revealed. I have no idea what she meant, but it seemed like a threat of some kind."

Trey put his arm around her shoulder. "Aunt Sarah is just being Aunt Sarah, honey. She's old and crotchety, and maybe she thinks she's still in charge. Forget it."

Clara sighed. "I know you're right. But it's hard to ignore her when I'm so nervous about publishing my memoir in the first place."

Chapter Seventeen
Success and Questions

The next morning the first shipment of her books arrived. The minute the Fed Ex delivery man drove off, Clara ripped open the cardboard box and tossed the bubble wrap onto the floor. Her memoir! She picked out one and held it up. Oh, the cover was just perfect! She inhaled the new smell of fresh print, then turned it over and read the blurb on the back. In the left corner was her photograph. *Oh my gosh, there I am!*

"Trey!" she shouted. "Where are you?"

She looked up as he came through the back door. "I was outside, fixing the fence."

She handed him a copy of her memoir. "Look! It's here!"

He grinned at her. "You did good, honey."

She felt as if she were dreaming. All at once she started to cry. She'd done it. She'd published a memoir, *her* memoir. Even Trey had tears in his eyes.

Later that day, Clara walked into Boswell's with 20 copies of her memoir in her arms, and a young, smartly dressed woman stopped her. "Are you buying all those books?"

Clara smiled. "Oh, no. These are copies of a book I wrote. I'm displaying them at the bookstore."

"What's it about?" the woman asked.

Clara caught her breath. "It's a memoir, about the funny adventures I had when I was growing up in a big family."

"Sounds interesting. I'd like to buy one."

"Really? You really do?"

"Yes, I really do," she said with a laugh. "Would you autograph it for me?"

Clara set the stack of books she was carrying on an empty table and asked the woman's name. When she opened her memoir to autograph it, her hand shook so badly she could scarcely scrawl her name.

She had just finished when another woman with grey hair and a wrinkled face picked up a copy from the table and asked her to autograph it. Both women then moved toward the cash register.

Stunned, Clara watched them, and then Barb appeared at her elbow. "I think you have a winner here. I haven't even put them on the display table yet and they're already selling!"

Clara caught her breath. All she could think about was how unreal this felt. Barb touched her arm. "I'd like to put copies in our sister store in Ashton. Could you order a hundred more?"

*　*　*

Dazed with excitement, Clara arrived home two hours later to find a message on the answering machine. "Call me," Aunt Sarah barked.

The minute she heard her aunt's voice, a shiver went down her spine.

"Miranda is having a family dinner tonight," Aunt Sarah announced when Clara dialed her number. "Could you and Trey pick me up?"

"Sure, Aunt Sarah, but I thought Miranda's family dinners were always on a Friday. It's only Tuesday."

"This is different," her aunt said.

"Oh? Why is it different?"

"You'll see. Pick me up at five."

Five minutes later the phone rang again. "Clara, it's Barb. It's only been a couple of hours and your books have sold out already!"

"They're really all gone? Holy cow!"

"You'd better order some more for your book signing," Barb said.

Oh, God, the book signing. Clara started to shake.

*　*　*

Aunt Sarah was standing on her porch, wearing a long bright blue dress and black shoes. Her oversized purse hung from her arm and she had a dour look on her face. "We have to go to Larry's house," she announced. "Joe's been there all day."

Clara and Trey exchanged glances. Trey then drove around the block to Larry's house to pick up the uncles. Uncle Larry had on the black hat he always wore, and Uncle Joe carried a bulky paper bag under his arm.

"I have it," he whispered to Aunt Sarah as he climbed into the back seat.

"Have what?" Clara asked.

"None of your beeswax, young lady," Aunt Sarah snapped.

Trey frowned and patted Clara's hand. When they arrived at Miranda's house, everyone piled out of the car in silence. Aunt Sarah and both uncles walked up the steps to the front door, but Trey lingered behind with Clara. "Something's going on," he whispered.

Yes, she sensed it, too. She wanted to turn around and go home.

Later, after all the excitement had died down, Clara wished she had done just that. In the middle of dinner, Aunt Sarah had grabbed her chest and slumped over her plate. Trey leaped up and started CPR while Miranda called 911, and by the time the ambulance arrived, Aunt Sarah was breathing normally.

Everyone else was a wreck. Uncle Larry and Uncle Joe couldn't stop talking about Aunt Sarah's weak heart, and Clara didn't stop crying all the way home.

Chapter Eighteen
The Book Signing

The afternoon of her book signing Clara was so nervous she stood in her closet for over an hour trying to decide what to wear. She finally settled on a lavender sweater set and black slacks. She added the pearl bracelet Trey had given her many anniversaries ago and then studied herself in the mirror.

I look exhausted! My editor was right. Writing is not for sissies.

Using Trey's furniture dolly, they moved the heavy boxes of books out to the trunk of the Volvo, and when they were loaded, Clara stood staring at them. Her stomach felt tight as she climbed into the car, and she found herself wringing her hands all the way to the bookstore.

After he parked the car Trey glanced sideways at her. "You okay?"

"No." Never in her life had she felt this frightened, not even on her wedding day 38 years ago when she and Trey had gotten married.

Inside the bookstore Barb greeted her and led her to a wooden speaker's podium equipped with a microphone. It faced rows and rows of folding chairs, which Clara tried not to look at. A beautiful flower arrangement of red and yellow carnations sat on a nearby table.

"Oh," she exclaimed. "How lovely!" She teared up and Barb quickly produced a Kleenex.

"Hold it together, Clara," she whispered. "Don't be nervous."

Don't be nervous? Is she kidding?

She dabbed at her eyes. Then people started to arrive in two's and three's. She saw Mollie, who waved and smiled and was then swallowed up by the crowd. So many people … Clara didn't recognize half of them!

Finally Barb stepped up to the microphone. "Please welcome first-time author Clara Perkins. Her memoir, *Little Girl in Red Shoes*, is a heartfelt work that explores growing up in a very large family. I'll let her tell you about it."

With a smile Barb handed her the microphone and stepped back. Clara swallowed hard. Oh, Lord, that was her cue to talk about her book. She raised the microphone with hands that trembled. Dozens of faces looked up at her, and her heart began to pound. She drew in an unsteady breath.

"Th-thank you all for coming this afternoon. As Barb mentioned, this is my first book. I began writing it a year ago when I started thinking about how I had grown up back in the fifties."

Her mouth was so dry she could scarcely speak. She paused to sip from the glass of water on the podium.

"I grew up in Lafayette, Illinois, and I was the youngest of seven children. When I was five years old my mother died suddenly and from then on I was raised by my father and my Aunt Sarah."

She went on to describe the house they had lived in, her two brothers and four sisters, and some of the adventures they had. "It was a magical time, full of picnics and birthday parties and trips to the zoo."

She paused for breath, glanced up, and nearly dropped the microphone. There was Aunt Sarah, standing in the back! She blinked and looked again. Sure enough, her aunt stood almost hidden between two tall shelves of paperback books. Her face was white and she was scowling.

For a moment Clara forgot what she was saying, but a woman in the third row raised her hand and asked a question. From then on, Clara answered questions from the audience and talked about her memories until Barb signaled her to begin signing books. She laid the microphone down and was dumbfounded when the audience started to clap.

Then people lined up with copies of her memoir for her to autograph, and they asked more questions.

"When did you start to write?"

"About a year ago," Clara answered. "When I started a new journal."

"Have you always known inside that you were a writer?"

She laughed. "Most definitely not. There were days when I wondered what insanity had led me to pick up a pencil!"

"How did you come to write a memoir?"

"Well," Clara said carefully, "over time my journal just started to grow. All of my children are married now, and I wanted to let them know what my life had been like when I was young."

Then an older woman asked, "If it's not too personal, could you tell us what happened to your mother?"

Before she could open her mouth she heard Aunt Sarah's voice from the back of the store. "Clara, don't you dare say anything!"

She caught sight of her sister Miranda hustling Aunt Sarah out of the bookstore, and with an effort she turned her attention back to the woman who had asked the question. "Well ..." She faltered. "I—I don't really know exactly what happened to my mother. I think she died in the hospital, but I never knew why. I was so young nobody ever explained it to me."

Someone laid a copy of her memoir on the table and she had to focus on the line of people waiting in front of her. She autographed books for two more hours, and then Barb announced that *Little Girl in Red Shoes* had sold out. Clara was drained, and her empty stomach was growling. She couldn't wait to get to dinner at Restaurante Italiano.

By the time she and Trey arrived, everyone was already seated. She took one look at the tables full of applauding friends and people from her church, even some parents and teachers she'd known from when her children were in school, and burst into tears.

When she calmed down and dinner was served, she noticed with a sinking feeling that the table she'd reserved for her family was empty.

Halfway through her plate of fettuccini Clara got another shock when Dr. Rothman suddenly appeared at her elbow.

"Surprise!" the doctor said in a loud voice. The room went quiet and Clara stared at her. What was Dr. Rothman doing here? She hadn't been invited.

"I told you I would help you," the doctor said, raising a glass of champagne. "I said you would be a success when you when you were in my office last week, remember?"

Speechless, Clara stared at her.

With a theatrical gesture, Dr. Rothman turned to the roomful of diners. "I'm a psychotherapist here in New Millhaven," she explained. "Clara is consulting me about her anxiety problem." She smiled at Clara.

Trey leaned forward and spoke in her ear. "That woman is your therapist?"

Clara nodded.

"You know it is completely unethical for a therapist to say anything about a client outside of her office?"

"No, I didn't know that," Clara murmured. "But I sure do now."

Chapter Nineteen
Confrontation

The next morning Clara marched into Dr. Rothman's office, but instead of taking a seat on the sofa beneath the window, she remained standing. Something in her face must have betrayed what was on her mind, because the doctor sank onto the leather chair next to her desk.

"Dr. Rothman," Clara began in a firm tone. "Just what did you think you were doing?"

"What do you mean?" The doctor reached for the yellow notepad on her desk.

"You know exactly what I mean," Clara said. "What you did at my dinner last night was completely out of line. There is such a thing as patient confidentiality. It is unprofessional to publicly reveal the identity of a client."

"I have no idea what you mean?" the doctor protested.

"Oh, yes you do. You know exactly what I mean."

Dr. Rothman's gaze wandered from her desk to the window and back, but she would not look at Clara. "Well, I just thought I would explain—"

"And," Clara interrupted, "for a therapist to say anything at all about the personal, private reason a client may be consulting them is not only unprofessional, it is unethical."

"Oh. Well, maybe I did say a little too much, but—"

"You said a great deal too much, Dr. Rothman. I am going to tell my physician what you did and ask him how to report your behavior to the medical licensing board."

Dr. Rothman stared at her. Suddenly she tipped her chair back and her pink tennis shoes lifted off the floor. "So now that you're a famous author, you think you can threaten me?"

"I am not a famous author. And this is not a *threat*. I am simply telling you that I am going to report your unethical actions."

"No one will take it seriously!" the doctor shouted. "No one will believe you!"

Clara looked straight at her. "Everyone will believe me," she said quietly. "Everyone who was at my dinner last night heard every word you said."

On her way out, she stopped at the receptionist's desk. "Dr. Rothman will not be billing me for this visit."

When she walked out of the building, Clara ran into her friend Mollie. "Mollie! What on earth are you doing here?"

"My new therapist has an office in this building. But you know, Clara, if this one doesn't work out, maybe you and I should just make a pact to meet every week for mental checkups!"

Clara peered at her friend. "You're not here to see Dr. Rothman, are you?"

"No. I'm seeing Ivan Slatera. He's new in town and my doctor recommended him."

"Well, good luck. I just walked out on Dr. Rothman."

Mollie gaped at her. "You did? But why?"

"You must know why. You heard her at the restaurant last night, telling everyone I was consulting her about my anxiety. That is completely unethical. I'm reporting her to the medical ethics board."

Mollie's dark eyebrows went up. "Oh, wow! Can you really do that?"

"I sure can. Mollie, think a minute. Don't you think it's weird that all the therapists I've seen in the last four months are crazier than I am?"

Mollie laughed and hugged her, and they arranged to meet for coffee on Wednesday. Then Clara got in her car and drove straight to Dr. Shu's office to tell him about Dr. Rothman's behavior.

Dr. Shu's waiting room was crowded, but when the receptionist heard the reason for her visit, Clara was quickly ushered into his office ahead of everyone else.

"Clara!" Dr. Shu offered her a seat and sat down across from her behind his desk. "What's this all about?"

She cleared her throat. "Remember Dr. Rothman? Teresa Rothman? The therapist you recommended?"

"Yes, I do. What seems to be the problem? Didn't it work out?"

"None of them have worked out, Dr. Shu. I can't believe how … well, really strange some therapists are."

"Perhaps you'd better explain," the doctor invited. He sat back and waited expectantly.

"The first therapist you suggested was Dr. Morrison, remember? Right away at our first meeting she started talking about all the books she'd written and the problems she had in her childhood and with her parents and how she'd traveled all over the world and on and on. I never got to talk about my anxiety."

Dr. Shu frowned and jotted something on a notepad. "Go on."

"After I left Dr. Morrison I tried another therapist, Renée Craig."

"What happened with her?"

"She had cats. And she lied about it."

"Oh, I see. I remember that you're allergic to cats. Highly allergic, as I recall."

"Dr. Craig swore she didn't have any cats, but I kept sneezing and sneezing and finally I discovered she had not one but three cats in the room next to her office. Of course I couldn't continue with her, but I was still having anxiety attacks so I tried out another therapist that a friend recommended, Dr. Timothy Stevens."

"And?"

"I saw him only once. He talked nonstop about his unhappy life with his parents, how he was forty-six years old and had just married his twenty-one-year-old wife and how difficult it was for him. I thought that was really inappropriate. Don't you?"

The doctor nodded. "Sure sounds like it, Clara. "Completely inappropriate."

She took a deep breath. "Which brings me to Dr. Teresa Rothman."

"Yes, I remember recommending her. What happened?"

"She turned up uninvited at a private dinner I arranged after my book signing, and announced to everyone that I was seeing her professionally about my anxiety problem."

Dr. Shu slapped down his pen. "Let me get this straight, Clara. Teresa Rothman said publicly that you were consulting her for anxiety?"

"Yes. That's why I came to see you today. I want to report her behavior to the appropriate ethics board, if there is such a thing."

"There most certainly is an ethics board," Dr. Shu said. "And you should definitely report this." He stood and walked to a filing cabinet and pulled out some papers. "Fill these out and give them to my receptionist. The board will contact you at some point, but I have no idea how long it will take."

"It doesn't matter," Clara said. "I want to do the right thing. Other people need to know about this kind of behavior."

The doctor smiled at her. "You know, in the last few months you have consulted four therapists about your anxiety attacks. It seems to me all four have just added to the problem."

"I don't know whether to laugh or cry," Clara admitted. "It was pretty awful trying to get help from any of them, but looking back on it now, I can see the humor in it. All the therapists I consulted needed therapy themselves!"

That night Clara climbed into bed next to Trey and mentally took stock of her feelings. She had published her memoir and weathered her fear of exposing herself in public. The book seemed to be doing well; the bookstore had sold out and Barb wanted a hundred more copies. And she was going to report Dr. Rothman's unprofessional behavior.

She edged closer to Trey and felt a huge weight lift off her shoulders.

*   *   *

The next morning at the post office Clara opened her first fan letter.

Dear Clara,

I read your memoir with great interest because I have a similar story, though I was the oldest in my family. Our father was in the Army, so we moved around the country a lot. It was hard, but now that I'm an adult, I look back on it fondly. I am lucky to have lived in different areas and experienced different cultures.

Your memoir was so easy to read; once I started I could hardly put it down. I just wanted to let you know how much I loved it. I feel you are a friend.

Sincerely,

Annie Camillo

P.S. I hope you will write another book!

Carefully Clara folded the letter back into the envelope and reached into her purse for a Kleenex.

Chapter Twenty

Accusations and Answers

"Clara, where are you?" Aunt Sarah asked.

Clara sighed. "What do you mean, where am I? I'm at home."

"I need to go to the doctor's today. Come and pick me up right away."

The phone went dead, and Clara blinked. *Did her aunt just hang up on her? Why is she giving me orders like this?*

She put the fan letter in her purse to show Trey later, climbed into the Volvo, and drove straight to Aunt Sarah's. When she turned the corner, she saw that both her sister Miranda's dark blue Lexus and Casey's Honda Accord were parked in her aunt's driveway. *Why did Aunt Sarah need me if my sisters were here?*

The minute she walked in the front door she saw that the living room was in complete disarray, and her aunt sat hunched on the sofa with a box of Kleenex beside her. Casey was patting Aunt Sarah's back and Miranda was pacing back and forth from kitchen to the living room. Uncle Larry and Uncle Joe sat silently on the love seat under the bay window.

"What is going on?" Clara asked.

For a moment no one said a word. Then Aunt Sarah sobbed out, "I've been robbed!"

Now Clara began to understand the mess in the room. "Did they take anything?"

"Yes," her aunt wailed. "They took it away, Clara. They took it!"

"Took what away? What are you talking about?"

"Whoever broke in took all her jewelry and her house keys," Miranda answered. "They even went down to the basement and rummaged through those big cardboard boxes."

Clara caught her breath. She knew what was hidden in the basement. "And?" she pressed.

"Well," Uncle Larry said after a moment, "Sarah had a rifle hidden down there." He sent his sister a worried look. "Sarah, I told you it was a bad idea to keep it. You should have gotten rid of it years ago."

Miranda gasped. "What rifle? Why does Aunt Sarah have a rifle?"

Clara's heart started to pound. It had to be the same rifle she had accidentally discovered that day when she'd tripped and fallen on the basement stairs. She studied her aunt, who covered her face with her hands.

Uncle Larry coughed. "Sarah, I think maybe you should tell them."

"Tell us what?" Clara demanded. She dropped to her knees next to her aunt. "It's all right, Aunt Sarah. Just tell us why that rifle is more important than your jewelry."

Her aunt unclasped her bony hands and touched Clara's shoulder. "I ... I was trying to protect you, Clara."

"Protect me from what?"

Aunt Sarah's face crumpled. "You mother made me promise never to tell you. And now the police will find that rifle and ... and …"

"And what? Whose rifle is it, yours? Don't you want it back?"

"Oh, no," her aunt exclaimed, swiping tears off her cheeks. "I never want to see it again."

Uncle Joe stood up and cleared his throat. "You'd better tell her, Sarah. It's been long enough."

"Tell me what?" Clara shouted.

Aunt Sarah gave a little choking sob and again touched Clara's shoulder. "Remember the day you were playing with Eileen Framer from the across the street? You were both only five years old, do you remember? You two played together all the time."

Clara nodded. Yes, she remembered Eileen Framer. They used to play hide and seek and they climbed trees in the cherry orchard. "What does this have to do with Eileen Framer?"

"Remember Eileen's father? He had an old white pickup truck," her aunt said in a choked voice.

"Yes, I remember. Eileen and I used to climb in and out of it and hide in the back."

Suddenly she remembered something else. The rifle! Eileen's father carried a rifle in the back of his truck. "Oh, my God," she murmured.

Aunt Sarah grasped her hand. "It was an accident, Clara. It just happened."

"What was an accident? What was it that happened?" She stared at her aunt's face. "It has something to do with that rifle you stashed away in your basement, doesn't it?"

Aunt Sarah gave a little cry. "One day you and Eileen got hold of that rifle, and you were dragging it across the middle of the street and ... and . . ."

"Oh, God. It went off, didn't it?" Clara covered her mouth with both hands. "The gun went off!"

"It was an accident," Aunt Sarah said, her voice breaking. "Eileen's father had just come back from a hunting trip, and in those days lots of men carried guns in the back of their truck. You had no idea that rifle was loaded."

Clara's mind went numb. What was Aunt Sarah trying to say? What did Eileen's father's rifle have to do with anything? "So," she said slowly, "Eileen and I were dragging it across the street and it went off. What happened then?"

Aunt Sarah looked up at her. "Your mother and I ran out to take the gun away from you, but it was too late. The bullet ... the bullet hit your mother," she wept. "They took her away in an ambulance and I put the rifle under my apron and hid it. I kept it hidden all these years because ..." She stopped and swallowed hard. "That rifle killed your mother, and you and Eileen had been playing with it."

All at once Clara felt cold all over. "Are you saying that I shot my mother? Why don't I remember that?"

"Because when your mother fell she bumped you into the street. You hit your head on the curb and it knocked you out. You were taken to the hospital, too, and you stayed there for two days with a concussion. But your mother ..." Her aunt broke into racking sobs.

Uncle Larry took over. "The police said it was an accident, but they searched the neighborhood and could never find the rifle. The Framers reported the gun missing, and a couple of months later they moved away."

Clara started to tremble. Both Miranda and Casey were crying. Clara stood up and faced her older sisters. "Do you remember any of this?"

Weeping, they shook their heads. "All Daddy said was that Mama had an accident and she was in heaven," Miranda snuffled.

Clara tried desperately to stay calm and think clearly. "Aunt Sarah, are you saying that I killed my mother? That all these years you have blamed me for Mama's death?"

"I thought I was protecting you, Clara."

"But it was an *accident!*"

"Sarah," Uncle Joe interjected, "stop and think a minute. If the police do find that rifle, they'll trace it back to the Framers, not to you. It doesn't matter that you've kept it hidden all these years."

"But," Uncle Larry interjected, "wouldn't that be considered withholding evidence?"

"And that," Clara said slowly, "is why you didn't want me to publish my memoir, isn't it, Aunt Sarah? You were afraid I would remember about Mama's death and I'd reveal that you took that rifle and hid it."

"Yes," her aunt said in a small voice.

Clara's voice rose. "And now that the rifle has been stolen, you're afraid the police will accuse you of having a gun in your possession that actually belonged to Mr. Framer."

Aunt Sarah said nothing.

"Aunt Sarah, I hate to say this to you because I've always loved you and looked up to you. You taught us to always do the right thing, remember? To always tell the truth, no matter how painful. But *you* didn't tell the truth, did you? All these years you kept my mother's death a secret. Even when I became an adult you never told me the truth."

"It was for your own good, Clara," her aunt whispered. "I was just trying to protect you."

"No, you weren't, Aunt Sarah. I was just a child. They would never hold a child responsible for what happened. They would consider it just a tragic accident." She paused to take a calming breath. "I think you were trying to protect yourself, Aunt Sarah. Maybe you felt you should have been paying closer attention to what Eileen and I were doing when we were playing in the street. Especially when we were playing with Mr. Framer's rifle."

Aunt Sarah's face was blotchy with tears. "I ... I know now that you're right. But back then I couldn't risk it. I was afraid you would be held responsible for your mother's death, and I worried about how that would affect you. I tried to protect you."

Clara just stared at her. "You were afraid my memoir would incriminate you for withholding information about that rifle from the police."

"Well, yes. Maybe I was wrong, but that is exactly what I thought."

"Oh, Aunt Sarah, I wish you could have just told me."

"I couldn't! I was afraid to tell you. I thought you would hate me." She sniffled. "You probably hate me now."

Clara sighed and once again knelt next to her aunt. "I don't hate you, Aunt Sarah. A person can be pretty angry at someone and still love them. But ..." She paused to steady her voice. "... I'm really angry that you raised such a fuss about my memoir. I felt enough anxiety for my own reasons, and you certainly added to it. I'm mad about that, but you're still my aunt, and I love you."

"Oh, thank God," Miranda said.

Uncle Larry stood, walked across the room, and took his sister's hand. "Sarah, do you have any whiskey in the house?"

Chapter Twenty-One

Red Tennis Shoes

Clara sat in the backyard without moving until Trey came home and found her. "Honey? What's wrong? You look like you've been crying."

She looked up at her husband. "I … um … have a situation." She took another swallow of the wine she'd poured.

"What is it? You look really tired. And it isn't like you to drink before dinner. What's happened?"

"Oh, Trey, it's a mess. A huge mess."

Carefully he lifted Clara's feet off the other lawn chair and sat down. "Tell me."

She drew in a ragged breath. "I found out today why Aunt Sarah and my uncles were upset about my memoir." She swiped tears off her cheek.

"Okay, why were they upset?"

"Because … because Aunt Sarah thought I was going to reveal something she's been keeping secret for fifty years."

"Yeah?" He lifted her wine glass out of her hand and downed a big swallow. "What was this secret?"

"When I was a little girl there was an accidental shooting in our neighborhood. Aunt Sarah hid the rifle that was involved."

"What? Someone was shot? Who was it?"

Clara concentrated on breathing slowly, in and out. "It was my mother."

Trey looked at her in disbelief.

Clara closed her eyes. "There's more. When I was little I had a friend named Eileen. One day we were playing out in the street with a rifle she found in her father's truck. Aunt Sarah and Mama saw us and ran out of the house, but before they could reach us the g-gun went off. The bullet hit Mama."

"And your mother died?" Trey whispered. "Oh, my God."

"I don't remember that part. But today Aunt Sarah told me that she took that rifle and hid it."

"That's the rifle you found in Aunt Sarah's basement," Trey said.

"Yes. Aunt Sarah kept that gun hidden all these years. She thought she was protecting me."

"And she never told you. You never knew what she'd done, or why she did it."

"All I remember is playing with my friend Eileen, but I don't remember anything else."

"How come you only found this out today?"

"Because last night Aunt Sarah's house was robbed and the rifle was stolen. She thinks the police will trace the gun to her, but she's wrong, isn't she? The rifle belonged to Eileen's father, Frank Framer."

Trey nodded. He started to say something and then snapped his jaw shut.

Clara bit down hard on her bottom lip. "I think I need to go to the police and tell them what I know."

Trey looked at her for a long minute, then strode into the house and came back with the bottle of wine she'd opened. Without a word he refilled her glass and poured one for himself. They sat together without talking until the sun sank behind the trees and darkness crept over the rose arbor.

That night Clara jolted awake in the middle of a mixed-up dream about her friend Eileen. She was wearing a yellow dress and dirty red tennis shoes.

Perspiration soaked her nightgown and her temples were pounding. She got out of bed and went into the kitchen for an aspirin and a glass of cold water.

There was Trey, sitting at the counter. He stood up and put his arms around her. "I guess you couldn't sleep, either."

Chapter Twenty-Two
Moving On

A week later, after she'd talked with the police, Clara woke up again in the middle of a nightmare about a little girl and a rifle. Trembling, she lay awake for hours thinking about everything that had happened. It felt unreal, as if she had dreamed it. As if it couldn't really have happened.

Carefully she slipped out of bed and tiptoed down the hall to the front room, where she sat staring at the clock on the mantel. She watched the hands tick inexorably forward, one second at a time, and a sense of helplessness flooded her.

There was no way to bring her mother back, no way to change what had happened or ease the guilt and sense of loss she felt. The clock struck three but she didn't move.

The next morning Trey found her asleep on the sofa. "You can't go on like this, honey," he said. "It's eating you up."

"I don't know what to do," she confessed. "I can't believe this is really happening. My mind won't stop asking questions."

After another week of sleepless nights she called Dr. Shu. When she spoke to the receptionist, she was put on hold, and in a moment the woman came back on the line. "The doctor wants you to come in right away."

She was dressed and ready in 15 minutes, and she barely remembered driving down the winding street to his office. In the waiting room she found herself staring at the oil painting on the wall; it showed a woman standing in a field of dry weeds, her dress and her long hair blown about by the wind. For some reason it made her want to cry.

"Clara," Dr. Shu said when she entered his office. "How are you?"

"Fine," she said automatically. Then she broke down. "No," she choked out, "I am not fine."

"What's wrong? Has something happened?"

She sobbed out the whole story, about her mother's death and Aunt Sarah and the rifle and going to the police and the nightmares she was having.

Dr. Shu listened and shook his head. "No wonder you're not sleeping at night," he said in a quiet voice. "This would be painful for anyone to process."

"I don't know why I'm having such a hard time. It all happened over fifty years ago. I don't even remember most of it."

"Clara, I don't think you ever told me about your mother. You were just five when all this happened, right? You've kept it buried for all these years."

"Until now," she wept.

"Until now, yes." He handed her a box of tissues and waited while she blotted her eyes, then folded his hands on his desk and studied her. She tried to smile at him. After a long pause he leaned forward.

"Do you know what I think you should do?"

She looked up at him. "What? Tell me."

"I think you need to talk to a therapist."

*   *   *

Later that morning she drove to The Tea Leaf to meet Mollie for coffee. When she arrived she sat in the Volvo for a quarter of an hour, trying to pull herself together. The people walking by looked as if they didn't have a care in the world. Would she ever feel like that again?

Mollie sat in their usual spot at the table by the window. "Clara, you look awful! What's wrong?"

Clara dropped into the seat across from her and put her head in her hands.

"Clara?"

"Just give me a minute, Mollie. I'll be all right when I have some tea."

Mollie rose from her seat and returned almost immediately with a steaming cup of tea. "Here. It's mint and chamomile. Very calming."

Clara wrapped both hands around the cup. "I'm not sure I can talk about this. I don't even know where to begin."

Mollie said nothing, just waited.

"You know about my Aunt Sarah, how upset she was about my memoir. That's what sent me into therapy, remember?"

"Yes, I remember. Didn't your aunt show up at your book signing?"

Clara nodded. "That's not the bad part."

"Okay," Mollie said. Her hazel eyes narrowed. "What's the bad part?"

"You're a good friend, Mollie. I don't know whether I can tell you about what's happened and make any sense."

Mollie reached over and squeezed her hand. "Try me."

She looked across the table at her friend. "Aunt Sarah has been holding onto a family secret for the last fifty years. She was afraid I had written about it in my memoir."

"What sort of secret?"

"It had to do with my mother's death, when I was five. I had a friend across the street. One day she found her father's rifle in the back of his truck and we were playing with it, and ..." She broke off.

"My God, Clara, what happened?"

Clara opened her mouth, but found she couldn't speak.

"Clara?"

"I'm still trying to get my mind around it," Clara said. "The day before yesterday Aunt Sarah told me about what happened, but it still doesn't seem real. I don't remember much about it, but what I do remember is that the rifle went off and ..." She gulped a swallow of her tea.

"And?" Mollie prompted.

"I want to tell you, Mollie, I really do. I need to talk it out with someone, but I just don't know how." She studied her friend's face and clenched her hands in her lap.

"The bullet hit my mother. That's how she died. I was playing with the gun that killed my mother! But I didn't remember that part of it until Aunt Sarah told me on Saturday."

"Oh, Clara, how awful for you."

"Aunt Sarah saw what happened, and she ran out of the house and got the rifle and hid it. She's kept that gun hidden in her basement all these years. Then when I wrote my memoir she thought I'd told about what happened. That's why she made such a fuss."

Mollie shook her head. "This would have me in therapy for the rest of my life!" She reached across the table and took her hand. "Clara, I think you need to talk to someone about all this. A professional."

Clara groaned. "Dr. Shu thinks so, too. But after all the bad experiences I've had with therapists in the past five months I'm not sure I can try it again."

"I think your doctor is right, Clara." Mollie tightened her fingers around Clara's. "I really do."

Clara stared at her. "You do? Honestly?"

"Yes, honestly. Listen, I've found a new therapist." She took out a business card and slid it across the table.

Clara studied it. "Is he …?" She hesitated. She wanted to say "ethical," but she rephrased it. "Is he any good?"

Mollie nodded. "I think he is very good. I'm finally getting some real help."

"I can't," Clara breathed. "I just can't."

"Clara, I think you have to get past this. You have to move forward."

She sat for a long minute, staring at her tea, and then at the business card Mollie had offered, and slowly pushed it back across the table.

"Mollie, I think I have this whole thing in perspective. In my heart, I know what happened was just a terrible accident. And you know what? I got through publishing my memoir and overcoming my fear of talking in front of a crowd of people, so I know I can get through this, too."

"Oh, Clara, I think you're absolutely right. You're a stronger person now. And I also think you are very brave."

They finished their tea and stood up to leave.

"You're a good friend, Mollie. I'm really glad we met." They hugged each other, and Clara watched her friend leave.

She glanced down at the business card still on the table, picked it up, and deliberately tore it in two. Then she dropped the pieces in the trash basket by the door and walked across the parking lot to her car.

THE END

About the Author

Erina Bridget Ring was born in New York and has lived in California for 38 years. Happily married for 40 years, she has raised three children and has four grandchildren. This is her fourth book. Other works by the author include *Knit 2, Purl 2, Kill 2: A Caretaker's Story of Survival*; *Breakfast with the FBI*; and *Diapers, Drama, and Deceit: The Mothers of Easthaven.*